Frank Boulderbuster – The Last of the Great Swagmen

Frank Boulderbuster is one of the last great swagmen – brave, bearded and fond of spinning yarns. He'll tell you the strange story of the smiling shingleback, the terrifying tale of the boxing ghost and all about the crazy caper of the Cologne Ranger.

He's known the length and breadth of Australia – from Adaminaby to Zanthus, from Poowong to Banunga. Whether he's dancing the famous spider dance, catching dangerous villains or braving the might of the Alice Springs Ladies' Club, there's no mystery too deep for Frank and his trusty owl, Frogwarble.

Also by Doug MacLeod

POETRY

Hippopotabus
The Story of Admiral Sneeze
Knees
In the Garden of Badthings
The Fed Up Family Album
Sister Madge's Book of Nuns

STORIES

Tales of Tuttle

EDITED BY DOUG MACLEOD

Kissing the Toad
and other stories
by young Australian writers

Frank Boulderbuster – The Last of the Great Swagmen

Doug MacLeod

Illustrated by Michael Atchison

PUFFIN BOOKS

Puffin Books
Penguin Books Australia Ltd,
487 Maroondah Highway, P.O. Box 257
Ringwood, Victoria, 3134, Australia
Penguin Books Ltd,
Harmondsworth, Middlesex, England
Penguin Books,
40 West 23rd Street, New York, N.Y. 10010, U.S.A.
Penguin Books Canada Ltd,
2801 John Street, Markham, Ontario, Canada L3R IB4
Penguin Books (N.Z.) Ltd,
182-190 Wairau Road, Auckland 10, New Zealand

First published 1985 by Viking
Published in Puffin, 1987

Typeset in 95% Caledonia by Leader Composition, Melbourne

Offset from the Viking Kestrel edition
Made and printed in Australia by
The Book Printer, Maryborough, Victoria

CIP

MacLeod, Doug, 1959- .
Frank Boulderbuster, the last of the great swagmen.

ISBN 0 14 032474 7

1. Children's stories, Australian. I. Atchison,
Michael, 1933- . II. Title.

A823'.3

To Michael Dugan

Contents

Introduction

'All swaggies are ratbags!' my mother would say. 'If that's a lie may lightning strike me down! You can smell 'em even before they hit town. They never wash, they never shave and they never work. You'll find them anywhere in Australia, from Adaminaby to Zanthus – dirty old blokes carrying their homes around on their backs. Just like snails they are. No quicker and no smarter.'

Then she would shake her finger at me and give me a stern warning. 'If ever you become a swagman, Frank Boulderbuster, I'll catch up with you and put jumping ants in your britches. I'll make you eat Kingaroy peanuts till you blow up like a cane toad, then I'll pop you with my hat-pin, or may lightning strike me down! All swaggies are ratbags! Be a Sunday School teacher Frank, like your mother!'

That was sixty years ago when I was a youngster in the New South Wales town of Triambelong. My mother would keep telling me how terrible swagmen were, so it was only natural that I should become a swagman myself. Not a dirty, lazy ratbag but a proud gentleman of the road. My mother never caught up with me as she had promised. One Sunday she told a lie and lightning struck her down.

I miss my old mother but most of all I miss the company of other swagmen. Nowadays, swagmen are as rare as emus' teeth. For all I know, I might be the only one still on the road. Just in case you never get to meet me, I've decided to write a book; a book about my life. Be careful with it now, and remember that every word in it is absolutely true, or may lightning . . . but never mind about that.

Your mate,

Frank

THE FLIES WERE GIVING ME A TOUGH TIME
WHEN I WALKED INTO CUNNAMULLA

The Smiling Shingleback

The flies were giving me a tough time when I walked into Cunnamulla. It was the middle of a Queensland summer. Dogs wandered around with their tongues dangling out and shingleback lizards, who loved to sunbake their stumpy tails, decided it was too hot even for them. The only animals which could move quickly in the heat were the flies, and there were enough of them to lift a chook-house door off its hinges. I tried shooing them away with my hat, but they only came back again. There was no point in wasting my energy. Besides, my old brown hat couldn't take much flapping about, since the brim had almost given way. The only thing to do in this heat was to find a pub.

Most of the Cunnamulla people were in the pub. It wasn't only the place where people drank beer, it was also a sort of trading post. People were trading anything of value for a glass of beer: clocks, cameras, clothes and big bottles of the local honey which was the best in Australia. All heads turned as I walked towards the bar.

'I'm busting for a beer!' I told the barman.

'You'll have to do better than that,' the barman replied. He looked thin and mean – not the sort of bloke to give free beers to swagmen. 'Got any money?'

'Not much,' I admitted.

'Anything to trade?'

That was a good one! Everybody knows that a swagman has nothing of value to anyone but himself. All I had were my old clothes, the rolled-up blanket on my back and some flour and jam. I didn't intend to give up the flour or the jam because they were for making jam damper, my favourite food. I might have died of thirst if it hadn't been for one kind-hearted old woman who bought me a beer.

'Is this your first time in Cunnamulla?' she asked.

I nodded, wiping the beer froth from my beard.

'Well, if you need anything, just come to me. I'm Ma Evans, and I have a soft spot for swagmen. You see, Frank, I'm a bit of a traveller myself.'

I was just about to ask Ma Evans how she knew my name when an enormous hand gripped my shoulder and spun me around. The hand belonged to a huge bloke who looked about as friendly as a mud-wrestler.

'Beefhead O'Brien's the name!', he bellowed. 'What are you doing in Cunnamulla, swaggie?'

I didn't want any trouble from Beefhead O'Brien. 'I was just having a drink with my friend here,' I said, though when I turned to introduce Ma Evans she was gone.

'Tell the truth, swaggie!' roared O'Brien. 'You're here for the Cunnamulla Shingleback Race, aren't you?'

'What if I am?' I said, not knowing what he was talking about.

'You might as well go back to where you came from!' he said, and thrust his big red face close to mine. 'Because I've got the best shingleback lizard in Australia!'

O'Brien could have bragged the horns off a buffalo. He went on and on about how his lizard was called Mongrel and how it was the fastest thing alive. He was boring me silly so I decided to play a little game with him.

'My Mongrel is so fast,' shouted O'Brien, 'he can run from Arrelumbercumma Hill to Alyukurlpykurlpy before you've even *said* it!'

'So what?' I smiled coolly. 'I have a lizard that's so fast, he can run from Yea to Yass before you've even *thought* of it.'

A silence fell over the pub.

'My Mongrel is so good,' bellowed O'Brien, 'he can run even faster on a wet track!'

'Big deal!' I said calmly. 'My lizard runs so fast on a wet track, I've entered him in the Sydney to Hobart yacht race.'

'My Mongrel can bend a horseshoe!' cried O'Brien, ready to explode.

'My lizard can bend a horse,' I replied.

'Mine can eat bullets!'

'Mine catches them.'

'Mine can chase cars!'

'Mine drives.'

'Listen, you blokes!' said the barman, and I'm glad he butted in because I was running out of amazing things that my lizard could do. 'The big race is tomorrow at two, so why don't you both save your breath until then?'

'I'll see you there!' I said, trying to sound confident. 'By the way . . . er, how much prize money is there?'

'There's no prize money,' laughed the barman. 'The winner gets a brand new cabbage-tree hat. Everyone knows that.'

Me and my big mouth. I had never owned a lizard in my life, let alone a shingleback that was supposed to be faster than a racehorse. But I was a swagman and a swagman never backs down on a challenge. Besides, a new cabbage-tree hat was just what I needed.

I sang softly to myself as I walked along the burning hot footpaths of Cunnamulla, searching for any shinglebacks which were silly enough to be sunbaking on the roadside.

'Shinglebacks are smarter than you think!' said a voice which startled me. Ma Evans had appeared from nowhere to join me on my lizard hunt. She was carrying a black leather bag which looked as though it had seen more days than my old brown hat. It was weird how that woman could appear and disappear in the blink of an eye. I figured the sun was slowing me down and it was taking me longer to blink than usual.

'Do you know much about shinglebacks?' asked Ma Evans as we plodded on.

'They're slow, bad-tempered and lumpy. What else is there to know?'

'Plenty. If you stroke their tails they can cure warts. They hiss loudest before a storm. They can see round corners and they bring you luck if you get the ticks out of their ears.'

'And how do you do that?'

'Smear a bit of vaseline over each earhole and the ticks come tumbling out. Guaranteed to bring you luck!'

'That's what I need at the moment,' I huffed. 'Trouble is, I can't find a shingleback.'

'There are other ways of getting luck, you know.'

Ma Evans suggested bathing in cold tea, jumping three times over an anthill and wearing inside-out clothes, which were all ways of changing bad luck to good. She would have come up with a dozen more if I hadn't stopped her by asking how she knew so much.

'I'm a traveller,' she explained. 'I go from door to door selling people remedies for everything from bad luck to toothache. Haven't you heard of Ma Evans' famous hair restorer? I make it from twelve different types of mud. Slap it on your bald head in winter and you'll have curls in the spring. Yes sir, I've travelled far and wide! I learnt how to cure lumbago in Pago-Pago, how to cure a stutter in Calcutta and how to stop the queasies in Zambesi.'

'You must have a cure for everything,' I said.

'Not quite. There's a witch in Tipperary with a cure for beriberi. I intend to visit her very soon. But there's still time for me to help you out.'

'I'm afraid I won't be able to pay you,' I warned.

'Of course you will! I don't expect money but I'm sure you'll be able to do me a small favour some time. Now, let me give you something!' From her battered black bag she produced two little rolls of paper, one red and one blue. 'Open up the red roll and read the message when you find your lizard. But don't read the blue message until the race is won.'

'That's all very well,' I said, pocketing the rolls, 'but how do I find my shingleback?'

'I have something else in my bag that will help. Have a look for yourself!'

'THERE'S A LITTLE BLOKE SHUT UP IN THERE!' I GASPED

She passed me the bag. Because I had expected it to be full of potions and powders, I was surprised to discover it was quite light. I opened it and peered inside. A little white face looked back at me and winked. I almost dropped the bag on my foot.

'There's a little bloke shut up in there!' I gasped.

Shaking her grey curls, Ma Evans took the bag from me, put in her arm and pulled out a little ball of white-and-brown-speckled feathers.

'This is Frogwarble,' she said, patting the feathers. 'She's my owl. A sort of travelling companion.'

The little owl looked at me with its huge yellow eyes and said, 'Boobook!'

'Frogwarble is a special owl. She prefers sleeping at night rather than during the day. With most owls it's the other way around. There's not much that escapes her sharp eyes. Here, you might as well hold her since you'll be working together.'

'What do you mean?' I took the owl clumsily but it remained calm in my hands.

'With her eyes, she'll find your lizard in no time at all! Let her sit in the crown of your hat. She likes that.'

'Are you sure you don't mind me borrowing your owl?'

'Why should I? Frogwarble likes you, I can tell.'

With a cry of 'Boobook!', Frogwarble flew off into the sky. I tried to spot her but was dazzled by the afternoon sun. By the time I could see properly again, Ma Evans had gone.

'Boobook! Boobook!'

The little owl's strange cry wasn't loud but it could travel a long way. I found her sitting on a fence post not far from the Cunnamulla pub.

'Don't fly off like that again!' I said sternly. 'Ma Evans

isn't going to be very happy if I lose you.'

As I picked up the owl to put her in the crown of my hat, I heard something hiss at my feet. For a moment I thought it was a tiger snake and I almost jumped out of my boots. Then I saw that the noise-maker was a genuine Queensland shingleback, resting in the shade of the fence post. Grabbing the lizard just behind the earholes, I lifted him up and had a look at the head of our future champion. He had the silliest face you ever saw – a broad, lazy grin with his tongue hanging out. It wasn't

I LIFTED HIM UP AND HAD A LOOK AT THE HEAD OF OUR FUTURE CHAMPION

exactly a winning smile but I decided then and there to call him Smiley. Then I remembered Ma Evans' two secret red and blue messages. I unwrapped the red note as she had told me to, but couldn't work out what the message meant:

Your champion you've found at last
But what will make him lightning-fast?
The recipe you now behold –
Feed your lizard liquid gold.

I had never heard of liquid gold before yet, according to Ma Evans' rhyme, it would make Smiley run fast. Liquid gold would have to be powerful stuff. Smiley was lazy, slow and stubborn. Even when Frogwarble tried hooting into his earhole to make him move, he didn't budge.

I sat under the shade of a wattle tree, resting my back against the trunk, and wondered what liquid gold could be. Perhaps it was a special formula that Ma Evans would sell me for a high price? The road was full of travelling tricksters who could talk people into spending money on potions which were only tap water. But Ma Evans was honest, I was sure of that. Liquid gold was probably just a fancy name for something ordinary; something I could find anywhere if I only knew what I was looking for.

When I tried to get to my feet again, I found that the rolled-up blanket on my back was glued to the tree with sap. In the heat the sap had oozed down the trunk. As I unstrapped my blanket and scraped off the sticky goo, Ma Evans' rhyme came back to me. The sap was golden and it was liquid enough to run down the tree trunk; was this the liquid gold that would make Smiley run lightning-fast? I scooped a little of the sap on to a twig and held it in front of Smiley's nose. He opened one of his sleepy eyes,then the other.

'Come along, boy.' I coaxed. 'Here's some nice tree sap for tucker.'

At last Smiley opened his grinning mouth. He popped

his tongue out and flicked a little ball of spit on to the sap. Then he went back to sleep. The great race was tomorrow and Smiley looked like being the biggest failure since my old mother's jam roll, which blunted three axes in the Bong Bong woodchopping event.

Never in the history of Cunnamulla had so many people flocked to see the Shingleback Race. From all over Queensland people arrived in their best clothes, hoping to see some action. They had all heard about the swagman who dared challenge Beefhead O'Brien. A special racecourse for the lizards had been staked out with tent pegs and string. It went right around the pub, a big wattle tree marking the start. Nobody expected the lizards to finish the course; the winner was simply the one who could crawl the furthest in fifteen minutes.

It was a sunny noonday when I arrived with Frogwarble perched on my hat and Smiley asleep in my pocket. Gentlemen in top hats and women with pretty umbrellas were watching the proud lizard-owners parade their pets. The eleven shinglebacks all had their numbers on brightly coloured silks tied to their backs. It could have been a racing carnival anywhere in Australia, except that there were no horses. Some people handed over their bets to the bookie while others made a bigshow of studying the lizards through binoculars.

'Number eight looks a bit frisky!' I heard someone say as number eight made a clumsy grab at a fly and missed.

'I wonder where that swaggie's lizard can be!' another punter said.

I felt a hand so heavy on my shoulder that it just had to be Beefhead O'Brien's.

'Lovely day!' I said.

'Don't rub it in!' grumbled O'Brien.

'All I said was, it's a lovely day.'

'Not for me. It's too hot and dry. Look at my poor Mongrel over there!'

He pointed out his lizard, which was bigger and uglier than all the rest. Mongrel's number was one. It suited him as he seemed to think he was the boss of the track. Numbers four, five and seven crawled past and Mongrel hissed at them furiously.

'Poor old Mongrel!' moaned O'Brien. 'He's not being mean enough. Before a race he usually starts biting the other lizards. But look at him now – he's as gentle and quiet as a baby.'

Mongrel spat at two of the other lizards. If this was Mongrel in a quiet mood, I prayed that Smiley would never meet him in an ugly one.

'It's this rotten dry weather!' cursed O'Brien. 'My Mongrel's a wet runner – he needs a wet track to win.'

'Tough luck!' I said. '*My* lizard runs like the wind, whether the track is wet, dry or on fire.'

Even the immensely stupid Beefhead O'Brien guessed that I wasn't quite telling the truth.

'Just where is this champion of yours?' he asked.

'Yeah, where is he?' demanded the barman, who was in charge of the race. He held a list of the lizards competing. On his clipboard were the numbers one to twelve. Only the number twelve did not have a lizard's name beside it.

'Don't worry!' I said. 'Just write Smiley alongside number twelve and bet your bottom dollar on him.'

I had less than an hour to find the liquid gold which would make Smiley a winner. I walked away from the jostling crowd to the back of the pub where it was quiet and I could think.

'Boobook!' said Frogwarble. Couldn't that bird say anything else?

'Hisssss!' said Smiley, as he woke up in my pocket. He was wriggling about so much it was an effort to grab hold of him.

'What's gotten into you?' I asked.

As soon as I put him on the ground he started crawling towards a rubbish bin at the back door. The lid was off so it was alive with flies attracted by the sweet smell of a few drops of rum left in an open bottle. Was this what had made Smiley so excited? To the annoyance of the flies I picked up the bottle. According to the label it was rum from the famous Queensland town of Bundaberg – and what was left in the bottle was dark gold in colour. Liquid gold.

'This must be it!' I whispered to Frogwarble. 'This is the liquid gold from Ma Evans' rhyme. It seems dishonest to give booze to a lizard before a race, but a few drops can't hurt.'

I tipped the dregs of the bottle on to Smiley's tongue. His eyes opened wide and his grin seemed to grow even larger than before.

'It's working!' I cried.

Suddenly his eyes closed again. A curious rumbling noise came from his grinning mouth.

'Listen to him, Frogwarble! He's roaring! That's the killer instinct building up inside him!'

Frogwarble, who was sitting on the rim of the rubbish bin, shook her head. Smiley's roaring was becoming very loud and regular, and soon I realised the truth.

'He's not roaring. He's snoring! That rum has put him to sleep!'

I may not have found the liquid gold but I learnt a valuable lesson: don't waste good rum on shinglebacks. Things had gone from bad to worse. It was impossible to wake Smiley and the race was due to start soon. This could be a very embarrassing experience. Crouching beside the rubbish bin, I wished that a garbo would come to collect me. I heard footsteps and peeped over the top of the bin to see Beefhead O'Brien and the barman. They had come here to have a private discussion. My blood froze when I saw O'Brien hand over a rifle to the barman.

'It's very simple,' said O'Brien. 'You fire this rifle to start the race. But make sure you aim for the water tank on the roof of the pub. That way, we'll get a shower.'

'I still don't like the idea,' said the barman. 'Somebody could get hurt. Why don't we use blank cartridges instead of real ones?'

'Because then you won't make a hole in the tank, will you, stupid?'

'It seems a lot of trouble.'

O'Brien suddenly puffed himself up like a great cane toad.

'I don't care how much trouble it is! I've bet a thousand bucks on Mongrel. He has to win this race and the only way to make sure of it is to wet the track.'

'But what about the tank? A busted water tank takes a lot of money to fix these days.'

O'Brien handed the barman a crumpled fifty-dollar note.

'And you'll get another one,' he said, 'when Mongrel wins.'

With that, the two bargain-makers went back to the crowd.

'I thought *I* was cheating!' I said to Frogwarble. 'Those two are downright crooked! We'll have to do something about it!'

At two minutes to two, we all placed our lizards behind the tiny starting gates. Some people looked disappointed when they saw how small Smiley was. It would have disappointed them even more to know he was sound asleep.

'Please stand behind the barriers, ladies and

gentlemen!' yelled the barman. 'This is a clean race so there will be no swearing, stomping on the lizards' tails or cheating of any kind.'

I saw him flash a sly look at O'Brien, who winked back. The bookie stopped taking bets and waited impatiently with the rest of us.

'The race begins as soon as I've fired this rifle,' announced the barman.

He pointed the rifle into the air. As the seconds ticked by he lowered the rifle so it pointed at the water tank on the pub roof. The barman, Beefhead O'Brien and I were the only people who knew foul play was going on.

'Five seconds to go!' called the barman. 'Four! Three! Two! One! *Ye-owww*!'

Frogwarble had crept up behind him and pecked him sharply on the ankle, causing him to miss the tank completely. Instead, he fired the rifle into the wattle tree overhead. Nobody knew that O'Brien's little plan had been foiled by Frogwarble, and the race started. Eleven shingleback lizards crawled awkwardly out of the starting gates, leaving Smiley fast asleep at gate number twelve. One lizard managed to get ahead of Mongrel and was bitten for his trouble. Even on a dry track Mongrel was going to be tough to beat.

'Come on, Smiley!' I shouted. 'Wake up, you dozy little coot!'

Beefhead O'Brien yelled something insulting at me. I couldn't hear what it was because there was a strange buzzing noise in my ears. Other people must have been hearing the same noise because they covered their ears with their hands. The buzzing grew louder and louder. Though the race was exciting, people were looking away to try and discover what was making the terrible din. Suddenly a mighty swarm of bees with their stingers at the ready flew out of the wattle tree. As mad as could be, they peeled off into squadrons and made dives at the people below.

'Head for the dam!' somebody yelled.

Not wasting any time, I joined the crowd as it stampeded down the hill towards the dam. With the fierce bees hot on our tails we jumped in, best clothes and all. Abandoned top hats and pink umbrellas floated alongside the bubbles from people who had disappeared below. Up and down we bobbed, gulping air and trying not to swallow any bees. Once I bobbed up for long enough to see the barman and Beefhead O'Brien rise out of the water.

'You drongo!' yelled O'Brien, gripping the barman by his fancy coat collar. 'You shot a beehive!'

Before he could say anything else a bee landed on his nose and he dived, quicker than a ferret down a rabbit hole.

Eventually the bees called off their attack. Covered in pond slime and the odd yabbie or two, the crowd climbed out of the dam. When we were certain nobody had been left on the bottom, we raced back to the pub to find out the winner of the Cunnamulla Shingleback Race.

All the lizards were exactly where we had left them. They were squirming around in something which looked sticky and syrupy. In trying to get free, they only became more gummed up in it.

Looking miserably at the waterlogged crowd, the barman declared the race a wash-out. There were grunts of disappointment. The bookie was starting to hand back the people's money when his sharp eyes spotted something.

'Look at number twelve!' he gasped. 'Number twelve is moving!'

People brightened up as Smiley crawled happily towards the sticky mess on the track. The silly lizard was going to get himself gummed up with all the others.

'Until number twelve gets stuck,' announced the barman, 'the race is still on.'

But Smiley had more brains than I thought. He sniffed the goo and looked up to see it falling from the wattle tree in sweet, golden drops. He opened his mouth wide and let the liquid gold fall on to his tongue. This was a real treat for a shingleback. With his belly full of honey, Smiley should have been even slower than before. But a change came over him. He slithered, then he trotted, then he galloped, then finally...

'He's up on his hind legs!' cried the bookie. 'That must be the fastest shingleback in history!'

Powered by the sweet golden stuff which had dripped from the tree, Smiley *ran* – not just once around the pub but again and again and again. He moved so fast that all you could see was a grey blur and beneath it, a groove in the ground becoming deeper and deeper. Beefhead O'Brien stared so much his eyes nearly fell out. People laughed themselves silly at the sight of this unknown lizard, charged up on a bellyful of honey from the broken beehive. For this was the liquid gold that Ma Evans had written about. Famous Cunnamulla honey.

When Smiley had completed the course for the fiftieth time, he decided it was boring just running around in circles. He ran up one side of Beefhead O'Brien then down the other. People cheered wildly as the grey blur that was Smiley headed for the dam, ran across the top, then disappeared over a hill. When he had gone there was a roll of thunder. Rain poured out of the sky, washing the honey off the racecourse, the mud off the people and the frown off Beefhead O'Brien. He joined us all in celebrating Smiley's victory. In the pouring rain we drank toasts to the many fine shinglebacks of Queensland, even Mongrel who was running like the champion he was, now that the track was soaking wet. But everyone agreed it was Smiley's race and they all showed their respect by being silent for the prize-giving

HE RAN UP ONE SIDE OF BEEFHEAD O'BRIEN THEN DOWN THE OTHER

ceremony. The crowd parted to make an aisle, down which the barman paced towards me. He was carrying a fine hat box which made a noise like a drum as the rain fell on it.

'To the new winner of the Cunnamulla Shingleback Race, may I present this handsome cabbage-tree hat,' the barman said gravely, handing the box to me.

The crowd held its breath. I opened the box and peered in. There at the bottom was a tiny cabbage-tree hat no bigger than a teacup. The barman was right. The hat was for the winner of the Cunnamulla Shingleback Race. It was just the right size for Smiley's head.

Unfortunately, we never saw Smiley after that day. But later in the afternoon the rain stopped and a beautiful rainbow stretched across the sky. Most rainbows have seven bands of colour but this one had eight. Besides violet, indigo, blue, green, yellow, orange and red, there was also a grey band which had never been seen before and has not been seen since. I knew it was Smiley running across the top of the rainbow to find a pot of liquid gold at its end.

It wasn't until the rainbow appeared that I remembered Ma Evans and her secret message. 'Don't read the blue message till the race is won,' she had said. I unrolled the blue paper and found another of her rhymes.

The race is won and now you know
That honey makes a lizard go.
A favour I have done for you
So payment unto me is due.
I've travelled far away to find
Strange learning of a magic kind
Till I return from distant lands
I leave my owl in your good hands.

Frogwarble flew down from out of the blue and landed on my hat. There she made herself comfortable. So this was the small favour Ma Evans had spoken about. I had to look after her owl for a while – maybe even a few years – the rhyme didn't say. But I was sure of one thing. When she wanted to claim her pet Ma Evans would have no trouble finding me. That woman had enough magic in her to track down anybody, even a swagman.

I soon forgave Ma Evans for tricking me into taking care of her owl. After all, Frogwarble was a handy mate to have. I was no longer troubled by flies, since she would either frighten them away or eat them. She became so used to sitting in the crown of my hat and I became so used to having her there, I knew I was stuck with that old floppy hat for good.

As for the tiny cabbage-tree hat, I keep it in excellent condition, waiting for the day I meet up with Smiley again. Somehow, I doubt that I ever will.

ONE OF THESE DAYS I PLAN TO WRITE A RECIPE BOOK

The Boxing Ghost

One of these days I plan to write a recipe book called *Frank Boulderbuster's One Hundred Amazing Things to Do with Jam and Flour*. It might take me some time because at the moment I can only think of one, and that is to make jam damper. Here's how you go about it. First, you mix some flour with water until it's all thick and doughy. To test the dough, roll it up into a fair-sized ball and shot-putt it at the nearest gum tree. If the dough sticks to the tree, it's just right. If it shakes the tree so much that koalas start falling out, your dough is too hard. If it splatters all over the place and dribbles down the trunk, your dough is too soft. When you have made sure that your dough is of the right thickness, roll it out into a long snake then wrap it around a green twig so that you have a long twisted piece of dough that looks like a barber's pole. Leave it in the embers of a fire and take it out when the dough turns black. Pull the green twig out of the centre, then fill the hole with jam. Eat it immediately. If you're really hungry, eat the twig for dessert.

My supplies for making jam damper were pretty low when Frogwarble and I arrived at Alice Springs. We had two dollars between us, which would have bought a jar of jam and a packet of flour, if only the shops had been open. Unfortunately it was ten o'clock at night when we hit the main street and the place looked deserted. The cruel cold of a Central Australian night was falling on the town and I felt grateful for the rolled-up blanket strapped to my back. If I couldn't find a roof for the night, at least I would be able to keep warm. The stillness was broken by the sound of a drunk singing *Waltzing Matilda* at the top of his croaky voice and laughing like a jackass. He came stumbling down the footpath towards me. Immediately, Frogwarble started hooting and shaking her feathers, which is an owl's way of saying that danger is approaching.

'Don't worry, mate,' I whispered to her. 'That bloke can't hurt us. He's as drunk as a camel at a christening.'

But something else had disturbed Frogwarble. There was a rustling noise in the shrubs beside the footpath, followed by a hideous, high-pitched scream. The drunk stopped in his tracks, about ten paces ahead of us. Even at this distance, I could see that he was quaking with fear as if he knew that something terrible was about to happen. Frogwarble hooted, the scream came again, then out of the bushes leapt a ghostly white figure wearing a shroud. It danced around on the footpath, howling in a voice like a peacock's, 'I am the boxing ghost of Alice Springs!'

The ghost reared up to its full height and towered over the poor sobbing drunk. If this really was a boxing ghost, then it was obviously a heavyweight.

'Strike me pink!' moaned the drunk.

'I'll strike you every colour of the rainbow!' sang the boxing ghost.

Hopping around like a champion, the ghost gave the drunk a punch right on the nose. The poor little bloke went cross-eyed, toppled down, then fell into a deep sleep. Showing incredible bravery for an owl, Frogwarble flew off my hat and started pestering the ghost by fluttering round its shrouded form. The ghost snarled and made clumsy grabs at the air. Even though I was a little put off by the ghost's fearsome display, I decided to give it a piece of my mind.

'Now listen here, you outback bogeyman!' I cried, pacing up to where it shimmered on the footpath. 'I don't care what sort of ghost you are, you shouldn't hit someone who's in no fit state to protect himself.'

'Gumnuts to you!' screamed the ghost.

Before I had a chance to move, I copped a wallop right in the belly which made me double up. That boxing ghost could certainly hit hard.

'Watch it, swaggie, or I'll give you a black eye too!'

'Not if I can help it!'

I DECIDED TO GIVE IT A PIECE OF MY MIND

Although I was in pain from the ghost's sneaky punch, I got in a fantastic left hook to the face (or where the ghost's face would have been if it had owned one) then followed through with a right uppercut to the chin. The ghost swept around in an agonised fury.

'I ought to sit on you for that!' it shrieked. 'But I have to go! Next time, swaggie, I'll flatten you!'

The ghost galloped off too quickly for me to follow it. Frogwarble flew off in pursuit but I called her back.

'Don't worry about hunting that ghost down tonight,' I told her. 'Even if you found it I'd be too whacked to do anything about it. We'll catch that ghost some other day – and when we do, we'll wallop it halfway into next week.'

This seemed to cheer Frogwarble up. After I had gotten my wind back I hoisted the poor unconscious drunk on to my back and carried him to the pub, where I knew I would find somebody to explain what had been going on. It seemed the best place to go.

The sign over the door read 'Boyle's Hotel – No Dogs Allowed'. Since it didn't make any mention of owls I figured it would be all right to take Frogwarble in with me. So, with Frogwarble perched on my hat and the sleeping drunk slung across my back, I made my grand entrance.

'Frank Boulderbuster's the name!' I cried to the late-night drinkers. 'Gentleman of the road and thumper of ghosts!'

I laid the drunk on top of the bar. There were murmurs of fear and pity from the sorrowful-looking customers. Now that I had a chance to take a good look at Boyle's Hotel, I noticed that the whole place had an air of misery about it. Nobody was telling jokes or making up tall stories, nobody was singing. Even the Queen's portrait hanging over the bar looked miserable, as if Her Majesty had just eaten a cucumber sandwich that was off. Bernie Boyle, the owner of the pub and chief barman, had a face that was longer than a basketball player's winter underwear.

'Poor old Cecil Gloomkisser,' moaned Bernie Boyle, pouring some iced water on the sleeping drunk's bruised face in an effort to revive him. 'Yet another victim of the boxing ghost.'

'You mean this has happened before?' I asked.

'He's the fourth one this week,' explained a sickly looking man who was propping up the bar. He punctuated everything he said by taking long sucks on a stinking corn-cob pipe. 'There was poor Barnie Howell – he got a busted jaw. Then there were the MacPhew twins – they copped a black eye each so we still can't tell 'em apart. And now, that rotten ghost's given poor Cecil Gloomkisser a squashed nose. Tell me, swaggie, did you actually see the ghost?'

'I did better than that. I punched it!'

'Good for you, swaggie!' cried Boyle. His customers seemed to cheer up at the news.

'Mind you,' I added, 'I copped a wallop so hard that I heard little birdies singing in my ears.'

'I don't want to alarm you, mate,' said the pipe-smoking stranger, 'but one of them little birdies is still on your head.'

'That's my owl. Frogwarble's her name.'

Frogwarble hooted in greeting.

'And I'm Dr Wingnut,' said the stranger, lifting his hat and revealing a bald head.

When I asked Dr Wingnut to tell me more about the curious boxing ghost he took a sad, long suck on his pipe, which gave him a fit of coughing. Then, with his red-rimmed eyes opened wide, he whispered, 'The boxing ghost is angrier than a Tasmanian devil and uglier than a moulting budgie. It's been plaguing the streets of Alice Springs for three weeks now – turning even the toughest late-night drinker into a gibbering nervous wreck. In all my years as a bush doctor I've never seen anything so awful! Most of the men in Alice Springs walk around in pairs nowadays. It's getting so as a grown drunk can't walk the streets alone at night.'

'The ghost only attacks drunks,' explained Bernie Boyle.

Since Dr Wingnut looked like the sort of person who'd be drunk most of the time, I could understand why he was so worried about the ghost.

'Never fear, Dr Wingnut!' I cried. 'I intend to get this ghost before I leave town. Nobody gives Frank Boulderbuster a bellyache without regretting it.'

I winced as the pain of the ghost's punch came back to me.

'You'd better give me a look at where the ghost hit you,' said Dr Wingnut. 'After all, I am a doctor.'

It didn't help my confidence to see Bernie Boyle trying to attract my attention by twirling his fingers around his ear and pointing his thumb at Dr Wingnut, suggesting that perhaps the bald doctor was a bit of a quack. Still, it would do no harm for him to have a look at my bruise, so I lifted my checked shirt and showed him my rock-hard stomach.

'You must be as tough as an overarm ten-pin bowler,' he marvelled. 'Most blokes of your age would be flat on their backs after receiving a punch like that.'

Suddenly I whipped my shirt down. A large lady had just stormed into the pub and I didn't want her to cop an eyeful of my belly. A swagman has his dignity.

'Hello, my little possum!' Boyle called to the newcomer. She must have weighed more than a camel with a dozen humps and she was anything but a little possum, but Dr Wingnut explained that she was Bernie Boyle's wife and that he often called her lovey-dovey names. Mrs Boyle grunted in reply to her husband's greeting.

'Did you have a good time at the Alice Springs Ladies' Club tonight, my angel-food cake?' Bernie Boyle asked.

'Yeah,' grunted Mrs Boyle.

'And what did you do tonight, my bush-baby?'

'Cooking.'

Besides being large and untalkative, another

interesting thing about Mrs Boyle was that she wore a huge piece of meat over her eye. I pretended not to notice it, since it would have been rude to make a fuss, though Bernie Boyle clearly felt he had a husband's right to know what it was doing there.

'Lovely piece of steak, my lamb,' he said. 'Is it a new recipe?'

'Nah. I got a black eye and I'm keeping it cool under this meat.'

Bernie's long face grew even longer. 'Don't tell me the boxing ghost got you as well?'

'Nah. Mrs Howell chucked a drop-scone at me.'

Everybody seemed relieved that the boxing ghost had not found its first female victim.

'You ladies ought to stop fighting with your food,' said Bernie Boyle. 'It's childish, and dangerous too, judging by the number of bruises you bring home from your cookery class.'

'But you must admit, my cooking's improved,' boomed Mrs Boyle.

'It would need to.'

'What did you say?'

'Nothing, my little witchetty grub. Nothing at all.'

As it was past closing time, the customers started to leave the pub in pairs. Dr Wingnut gave me his address and mentioned that he hoped to see me again. Then he walked out into the cold night, making such a smoke-screen with his corn-cob pipe that even the cleverest of ghosts would have had trouble seeing where he was.

Deciding it would be best to spend the night in the pub (Bernie Boyle said I could stay there for free if I got rid of the ghost), I gave Mrs Boyle my breakfast order – some jam damper, a cup of tea and a saucer of flies for Frogwarble. Then I dozed off and dreamt about the time I shadow-boxed with Les Darcy, the second-greatest Australian boxer who ever lived.

The next morning I felt an even bigger pain in my belly. It wasn't the boxing ghost's punch – it was Mrs Boyle's breakfast. Her jam damper was like a mallee root, her tea could have been sheep-dip and even Frogwarble's flies were underdone. If Mrs Boyle's cooking had improved since she started taking night classes, I hated to think what Bernie must have been eating for all those years before. Despite Bernie's advice I took my aching belly to Dr Wingnut's place. The bald quack was still smoking his corn-cob pipe even though it was nine o'clock in the morning. Frogwarble perched herself out of the smoke's reach, on a skull that rested on an empty beer bottle.

Dr Wingnut examined me and said, 'You're suffering from what we doctors call a gutsache.'

The pain was terrible. 'Is there any cure?' I asked.

The doctor shrugged his shoulders. 'How should I know?'

'Haven't you got any tablets or anything?'

'Try these,' he puffed, handing me a packet of pills the size of ten-cent pieces. 'They're for camels.'

'Camels?'

'And gutsache,' he added.

I chewed on one of the monster pills. It tasted even worse than Mrs Boyle's cooking.

'What's in these things?' I gasped.

'Sugar, eucalyptus, distilled mountain water and camel spit.'

'Eh?'

'Mostly camel spit,' he admitted.

I don't know how, but the pill worked. In fact, it filled me with energy and made me feel better than ever. Before I could express my gratitude Dr Wingnut said, 'No need to thank me. Just pay me.'

I didn't like the sound of that. 'How much?'

'For you, two dollars.'

'I don't have the money right now,' I said, 'but I'll pay you in the pub tonight.'

'I'm not going to the pub tonight. That ghost has scared me off, I don't mind telling you.'

'Suppose I get rid of the ghost this evening?' I suggested.

'Then you'll be my hero,' said Dr Wingnut. 'And you shall have as many free camel pills as you can eat.'

'That seems like a fair deal,' I said, taking the bag of pills and stuffing it into one of my pockets.

Dr Wingnut attempted to bid me farewell but he breathed in too much smoke from his pipe and had an attack of coughing and sneezing.

'Don't forget to take your blooming owl with you,' he spluttered. 'I think I'm allergic to it.'

Exercise. That was what I needed if I was going to beat the boxing ghost at its own game. Not far out of Alice Springs I found a spot which looked fairly deserted. It was a gap between two big red stone ridges – Simpson's Gap it was called. Here I could train without being watched by annoying sticky-beaks.

I unstrapped the blanket from my back, took off my coat and stripped right down. Proper athletes had special training shorts, but I had to make do with my underwear. First of all I did some stretching exercises so I wouldn't strain my muscles when it was time for the real hard work. I bent over backwards till I looked like a horseshoe, then did a double reverse-roll. When I had worked up a good sweat I started on the serious exercises like push-ups, sit-ups and burpees. Frogwarble watched me and even tried to copy some of my movements but, being a round sort of owl, the only thing she was good at was tumbling. This soon made her so giddy that she decided it was much more sensible to sleep instead. But sleeping was the last thing I wanted to do.

Now that I was getting really hot and sweaty in the

noonday sun, I started on the extremely difficult Frank Boulderbuster exercise program, a famous technique which involves waddy-chucking, yonnie-juggling and noggin-digging. Waddy-chucking is stick-tossing, yonnie-juggling is when you juggle with stones and noggin-digging is what it sounds like – digging in the sand with your head. Finally, I had a few rounds of shadow-boxing. This is a way of putting in some boxing practice when you're on your own. You pretend there's a boxer in front of you and you try to outwit him with fancy moves. If you get knocked out, it's best to think about taking up a different sport. I remember one day I gave my shadow such a boxing that it disappeared for three hours, even though there wasn't a cloud in the sky.

All of this can look pretty peculiar to someone who's not quite sure what you're up to. So concerned was I with building up my body that I didn't realise I had an audience – not until I heard cheering and wolf-whistling coming from the bank of the dry water hole at the foot of Simpson's Gap. I blushed like a beetroot. There was the Alice Springs Ladies' Club having a landscape-painting class. They were sitting at their easels, watching me cavorting in my underwear, right in the middle of their landscape. The loudest, longest whistler of all was Mrs Boyle.

'Wotcha doin', swaggie?' she called.

I stammered something about training as I hid behind a tree and pulled on my trousers, coat and blanket.

'Reckon you'll get the boxing ghost?' cried Mrs Boyle.

'Sure as you can wink!'

And Mrs Boyle gave me the sort of wink which didn't look at all decent to a bloke who was only half-dressed.

That evening I chatted with Bernie Boyle before going out to seek the ghost.

THERE WAS THE ALICE SPRINGS LADIES' CLUB HAVING A LANDSCAPE-PAINTING CLASS

'Have another beer?' the long-faced Boyle croaked.

'No thanks.'

'Go on. You might as well. There's nobody else here to drink it.' He picked up one of the towels from the bar top and wrung it out into a whisky bottle, which he put back on its shelf. 'Even the wife's out at school tonight. Another cookery class. Go on, have a drink with me.'

I was Bernie's only customer. Every drinker in town was too terrified of being punched up by the boxing ghost to go out after dark.

'If I'm going to net that ghost,' I said, 'I've got to be stone-cold sober.'

'Then I wish you luck,' said Boyle grimly, as I strode out into the mysterious night. 'You're a brave bloke.'

Frogwarble, as alert as ever, hooted from the top of my hat.

'And your owl's a brave bloke too,' added Boyle.

A full moon bathed the streets in an eerie blue light. Every dark corner and alleyway looked as though it might conceal the hideous boxing ghost, ready to spring and rain down punches on its luckless victim.

'Boobook!' Frogwarble cried into the night and was answered by another cry like her own, only deeper.

'Boobook!'

Was this another owl calling to Frogwarble, or was this the boxing ghost trying to lure us into a trap? We walked along the footpath in the direction of the noise. I remembered that the ghost would only attack drunks so I did my best to mumble and stagger as much as I could. At one stage, I even tumbled into some bushes. I cried out as I felt them claw me, expecting to have the ghost's fists pounding down upon me at any minute, but I managed to struggle free with only a few scratches.

'Boobook!'

The echo of Frogwarble's voice reached us again. Whatever it was, we were getting closer. Up ahead was a shelter where people could find relief from the afternoon sun. It was surrounded by bushes, any one of which could have been the white, shimmering maniac's hiding place. Forming my hands into fists but still pretending to be drunk, I shambled up to the shelter, keeping an eye on the bushes. Suddenly, they rustled wildly and there was an unearthly howling noise. My heart pounded like a pile-driver. I raised my fists. Out of the bushes darted two stray cats which had been having a scratch-fight.

I became a little more relaxed and wandered into the shelter. The ghost wasn't there. A rustling noise on the roof made the hairs on my neck rise, till I realised it must have been the branch of a tree rubbing against the corrugated iron. There was nothing to be afraid of.

I moved out of the shelter. Immediately, I was deafened by a scream from above. I looked up to see the boxing ghost diving from the roof towards me. There was just enough time to move aside, though the falling ghost still gave me a nasty knock on the shoulder. It was enough to make me really annoyed. Frogwarble screeched and the ghost cackled in triumph.

'Put 'em up, swaggie!'

'With pleasure!' I replied, more sober than I'd ever been in my life. We circled about for a few seconds, then started cuffing each other. The ghost's footwork was excellent and it ducked half my best blows. Worse still, while it ducked it usually managed to get in a really sneaky whack to my stomach. Soon I grew familiar with its tricks and started weaving and winding in a brilliant display of boxing skill. I made myself into a human tornado, my fists outstretched and my body spinning towards the ghost. I knocked it for six. But the ghost had an even shorter temper than me. With a shriek of anger, it bounced up and got me right below the belt. It hurt like mad but the ghost didn't seem to mind breaking the rules. It squealed with ghoulish laughter and raced off into the night.

Five minutes it took me to recover. In that time the ghost could have gotten anywhere. Fortunately, Frogwarble had flown off after my attacker and her hooting cry soon reached my tingling ears. I found her at the dark and gloomy Alice Springs school where she was perched on the roof. She stood out like a gargoyle against the full moon.

'Is the ghost here?' I whispered.

Frogwarble hooted softly and swooped down on to my hat. I prowled the schoolground for a few minutes, glancing in sheds and bike racks, but the ghost was nowhere in that dim, silent place. It was very peculiar. Bernie Boyle had told me that his wife was at a cookery class at the school, but the place was stiller than a tomb.

The only place I hadn't looked in was the big classroom itself. To my surprise, the huge wooden door creaked open when I pushed it. In the small beam of moonlight that shone in, I could see that the desks had been joined together to make a long bench on which were piled packets of flour and mixing bowls. A smell of hot damper filled the air. Cookery had been going on, but where was the cookery class?

Frogwarble fluttered around and made excited hooting noises. I fumbled for the light switch and flicked it. Everything was bathed in bright light – especially the row of white figures who stood with their backs to the blackboard. Facing me was not one, but a total of six boxing ghosts.

'Get him!' screamed the largest of the ghosts.

The line marched towards me, a hideous ghostly army ready to pound me to meat paste. I backed away, hoping to bolt out of the door and make a hasty retreat. But the door was shut behind me and I knew that the fearsome line of ghosts would circle me as soon as I tried to escape.

I was trapped. The ghosts moved closer and closer and closer. Quaking, I rummaged through my pockets, but there was nothing there to arm myself with; nothing except Dr Wingnut's crumpled bag of camel pills. I held out the six enormous pills in my hand, thought about throwing them at the six ghosts but decided to swallow them instead. I gulped. Half a dozen explosions went off inside me and I was gripped by an amazing feeling of strength. I felt as though I could crush Ayers Rock between my knees. I was invincible!

All at once the ghosts leapt on to me, trying to bamboozle me with sly punches. But I blocked them on all sides, spinning and twisting like a snake on a barbecue. Then I struck out.

CLANG! Ghost number one went flying into some pots and pans.

FWUMP! Ghost number two landed head-first in a sack of flour.

WHIZZ! Ghost number three went for a slippery-slide on a slab of butter.

SPLAT! Ghost number four sat in a bowl of eggs.

CLOMP! Ghost number five got brained by a sack of spuds.

That only left ghost number six. Even with my new super-strength, I was outmatched. Right punch, left punch, right punch, left punch – the ghost wasn't even getting tired. This was obviously the genuine boxing ghost; the terror of Alice Springs; the bogey that made grown men afraid to go out at night.

'Had enough swaggie?' guffawed the ghost.

I was going down fast. Everything seemed to blur. In the haze I saw Frogwarble fluttering overhead, carrying a little brown bag in her claws. I was ninety-nine percent unconscious when I saw her drop the bag on to the ghost. A black cloud appeared from the bag as it tore open; a cloud that found its way into my nostrils, making my nose tickle and burn like mad. Tears streamed down my face. It was pepper, and it was having a surprising effect upon the ghost. I watched through tearful eyes as it whined and howled and caterwauled.

'Ah... ah... ah...' gulped the ghost.

Finally, it sneezed a sneeze so enormous that the shroud it was wearing blew straight up to the ceiling and got caught on one of the rafters. It dangled down like a double-bed sheet – and that was exactly what it was. Beneath it stood the unmasked boxing ghost – Mrs Boyle – with her face red from the almighty sneeze.

'So you're the terror of Alice Springs!' I cried.

Sniffing, Mrs Boyle nodded. 'And these are my helpers – Mrs Howell, Mrs Wingnut, Mrs Rose, Mrs Ali and Mrs Cooper.'

The other ghosts in the room took off their bed sheets to reveal the Alice Springs Ladies' Club.

I SAW FROGWARBLE FLUTTERING OVERHEAD

'Aren't they little beauties?' said Mrs Boyle with pride. 'I've been training 'em.'

'But why?'

'Use your brains, swaggie!' said Mrs Boyle. 'This is the only way we can get our husbands to stay away from the pub. We scare 'em witless. Now they spend their nights at home.'

'What's the good of that,' I asked, 'if you're always out prancing around in your ghost costumes?'

'There's six of us so we work a roster, Monday through Saturday. That way, each of us only has to go out one night a week.'

'What about Sunday?'

'The pubs are closed, you drongo.'

There was one more thing I wanted to know.

'In all my years of boxing experience,' I said, 'I've never been hit by boxing gloves that were as hard as yours. Where do you get them?'

Mrs Boyle's red face turned a nice shade of pink as she smiled 'We bake 'em in our cookery glass. They're made of damper!'

My belly rumbled and I suddenly realised why I had gotten such a bad gutsache after eating Mrs Boyle's home-cooked breakfast.

'It was a good plan,' I said, 'but I've got a better idea.'

'Then let's hear it!' Mrs Boyle slapped me on the back so hard that the six camel pills I had swallowed almost popped up again. 'Any swagman who's smart enough to uncover the boxing ghost of Alice Springs is smart enough to solve our problems!' I told them my brilliant plan.

Things in Alice Springs have changed now that the boxing ghost no longer stalks the streets. Do you think the drinkers ever found out that Mrs Boyle had been behind it all? Of course they did – she told them herself. She also told them that from then on they had to let their wives and kids come to the pub with them and that they were allowed only two glasses of beer and no more. Anyone who didn't like this new rule could complain to the Alice Springs Ladies' Club and get two black eyes along with their two beers.

Of course it was all my idea, and if you think it was rough on the blokes, let me tell you, they didn't take it so badly. You see, the pubs in Alice Springs now open on Sundays, and they're famous for having the biggest beer glasses in Australia. If you don't believe me, go to Boyle's pub. You can't miss it because there's a huge painting by Mrs Boyle hanging over the bar – a landscape with figures, you might call it. The landscape is Simpson's Gap and the figures are an owl and a certain famous swagman in nothing but his underwear.

'BOULDERBUSTER'S COME BACK!' ROARED
A HUGE WRESTLER OF A BLOKE

The Galvons

A hundred galvanised-iron roofs reflected the brilliant orange of the setting sun as I strolled into Triambelong. Three old crows sitting on a galvanised-iron billboard cawed lazily at the end of a New South Wales summer day. Triambelong is famous for two reasons. It is the town where the best galvanised iron in Australia is made and it is also the place where I was born and brought up.

Memories of childhood flooded back to me as I wandered past the galvanised school with its galvanised playground. There was the corrugated-iron slide which used to thump hell out of our backsides as we slid down it. Beside it was the roly-poly iron tank where I used to tumble with my grade-four girlfriend, Piggy Ironpot. Further up the road was the church of iron which had been my Sunday school. I remembered the time that Piggy Ironpot and I played Mary and Joseph in the Sunday school concert. One of the three wise men had deliberately stepped on my robe so that it ripped, leaving me half-naked. Piggy Ironpot felt so sorry for me, standing there in my underwear, that she punched the giggling wise man, stole his gold and gave it to me.

Everything was as I remembered it, except that the

place was quieter than a cheer squad at a nuns' tiddly-winks tournament. Where were the blokes from the ironworks? Where was Baron Herbert, Triambelong's famous garbage collector who did his rounds in a frock and was so strong that he tossed the empty bins to the tops of the paperbarks? Where was the Triambelong Country Women's Association, renowned for its weekend outings to collect wild flowers and blow up abandoned cars? Where were the children of Piggy Ironpot's kindergarten class, the only children ever to steal a tuck-shop?

'Coo-ee!' I yelled.

Frogwarble hooted and the three crows cawed in reply but there were no people to greet us. I knocked on a few doors – they remained shut. The only place I hadn't looked was the ironworks, where the annual Iron Ball was held. The huge factory seemed perfectly still. There was no clangour of heavy machinery and no smoke coming from the chimneys. But as I got closer I heard the sound of a bush band. There was also the cheering noise of people celebrating.

'It's Boulderbuster!' someone cried as I approached.

'Boulderbuster's come back!' roared a huge wrestler of a bloke who could only be Baron Herbert. He lifted up his ball gown to come running towards me.

'Out of my way, Baron Herbert!' yelled Dynamite Doris, the chief car-exploder of the Triambelong Country Women's association. 'I want to be the first to give our Frank a hug!'

Doris grabbed me and squeezed me so hard that I was squashed out of shape.

'Look! He's got an owl with him!' screeched the kindergarten children.

They climbed up on my back to get Frogwarble down from my hat; the little owl hooted happily when she found herself the centre of attention. There were so many familiar hands to shake, I just kept moving my arm up and down like a pump handle. When I got to Baron Herbert he gripped my hand and shook it so hard that I was bounced up and down till a fair-sized hole appeared in the red soil at my feet.

'You haven't lost your touch, Baron Herbert!' I groaned. 'Are you still tossing rubbish bins to the tops of paperbarks?'

'Nope,' he said in his deep, husky voice. 'I thought it was time for a change. Now I'm trying to land a petrol drum on the steeple of the church of iron.'

'Not if I can blooming help it!' roared the Reverend Judas Smog, the most foul-mouthed bloke ever to get a job in the church. 'If I see a blasted petrol drum on top of my flaming steeple, I'll use your ears for organ-stops.'

Not wishing to create further argument, I complimented Baron Herbert on his dress.

'If I don't try something different now and then,' he said, 'I'll end up being as boring as one of Reverend Smog's sermons.'

Baron Herbert spent half his life trying to be different. The rest was spent starting arguments with the Reverend Smog.

'You great hardboiled lump of gristle!' cried the Reverend. 'There's nothing wrong with my blinking sermons! You're just too blooming thick to appreciate the beauty of the flipping English language.'

Before they came to blows they were quietened down by Ernie Slag, the factory manager. Ernie was as big and strong as Baron Herbert, but he preferred a gentler approach. He was famous for his black rum punch, the only drink in the world which can power an aircraft-carrier.

'Now, now, you two!' said Ernie, pushing the two enemies apart. 'I'll have no fisticuffs in front of my factory. Not when our old mate Frank Boulderbuster is here.' He turned to me and said 'It's a pleasure to see your whiskered face again, Frank! Won't you come in and have a drop of my black rum punch? There's a lady who'd like to dance with you!'

I could guess who the lady was, but I couldn't understand why the town was celebrating.

'It's a bit early for the annual Iron Ball, isn't it?' I said.

'We decided to have it now,' said Ernie, 'because there won't be any more Iron Balls, ever.'

Everybody suddenly became quiet. The kindergarten children who'd been making a fuss of Frogwarble looked glum. Dynamite Doris sniffed into her hankie. Strangely, Baron Herbert and the Reverend Smog had disappeared, possibly to fight a few rounds.

'I'm sorry you had to be the last Triambelong person to find out,' said Ernie.

'To find out *what*?' I asked.

'We're all finished,' said Ernie, sadly. 'Triambelong is dead.'

It came as a shock to me. I felt as if I had received a terrible blow. Suddenly, I realised I *had* received a terrible blow. For some reason, a flying rubbish bin had decided to make a crash-landing on my head.

There is nothing strange about a town dying. It happens all the time in Australia. Every town is built for a reason, and when that reason disappears, so does the town. It becomes a ghost town, with empty buildings and houses that gradually fall to pieces. Triambelong had been built because of the wonderful iron ore in its soil. The town had thrived on the ore, making famous galvanised iron to provide roofs, tanks, spouts and guttering for Australians. But now, every last bit of ore had been mined. Triambelong was doomed. It was a miserable thought. To raise everybody's spirits, Ernie Slag had arranged the party in his closed-down ironworks.

I woke on the factory floor, my aching head being cradled in somebody's arms.

'Cripes!' I heard Baron Herbert say. 'He's got a lump like a mullock-heap on his forehead.'

'Well, if you hadn't decided to chuck that flaming rubbish bin over the blinking factory roof,' roared the Reverend Smog, 'this wouldn't have happened.'

'Why, you bluffing, blustering blister on the backside!' huffed Baron Herbert. 'You were the one that bet me five dollars that I couldn't do it!'

'Swizzle, wangle and downright bulldust!' cried Smog. 'A blooming gentleman of the church like me doesn't gamble!'

'Oh yes you do, you oily old snake!'

'Want a blinking bet?'

'All right, all right,' said Ernie Slag. 'I think you two warmongers owe Frank an apology.'

'I'm sorry,' mumbled Baron Herbert.

'That goes for me too,' said Smog. 'In fact, we're so sorry, we're going to give you the money we bet.'

'Hang on!' grumbled Baron Herbert. 'I won that bet fair and square!'

The Reverend Smog gave him a warning glance and Baron Herbert grudgingly handed me two crumpled five-dollar bills.

'Lucky you, Frank!' smiled Smog. 'Now you'll have something to put in the collection plate when you come to my sermon tomorrow.'

'If you two keep this up,' said the person cradling my head, 'he won't *be* here tomorrow.'

I glanced up to see the round face of Piggy Ironpot, Triambelong's kindergarten teacher and my grade-four sweetheart.

'Hello, Piggy!' I said. 'How are your kindergarten kids?'

'Monstrous as ever!' she said. 'There they are, feeding rum punch to your owl!' Suddenly she cried out in a voice that almost deafened me, 'Raymond Goolie, stop putting Lindy in the punch! She'll ruin the flavour!'

Little freckle-faced Raymond let go of Lindy's legs and

'RAYMOND GOOLIE, STOP PUTTING LINDY IN THE PUNCH!'

went back to squeezing sauce in ladies' handbags.

'The poor little devils will have to leave Triambelong soon,' said Piggy. 'They can't grow up in a dead town, can they?'

'Don't think about that,' I told her. 'What about giving your brats a dancing lesson? We can show them how to do the barn dance!'

Arm in arm, we made our way to the dance floor. Piggy was an ideal partner for me, since we were the same size and equally light on our feet. Unfortunately, we were doing the sort of dance where we had to change partners every minute or so. My next partner was Baron Herbert, who gripped me so hard and kicked so high that he almost split his dress. We changed partners again. Baron Herbert moved on to dance with the Reverend Smog and the two of them somehow managed to twist each other's arms and kick each other's shins whilst keeping perfect time. I was doing my best to dance with little Lindy, who was dripping wet with the punch that Raymond Goolie had slopped on her.

We changed again. This time I was dancing with somebody I hadn't met before. She was an excellent dancer with dainty legs, red hair and big gold gypsy earrings. As we stepped and kicked, she introduced herself as Beryl Flynn. She pointed out her husband, Fiery Flynn. Like her, he had red frizzy hair and excellent dancing legs. At that moment he was showing Piggy a thing or two about barn dancing. The music ended and the dancers returned, exhausted, to their seats.

'Ladies and gentlemen!' cried Ernie Slag, 'I am pleased to announce that we have some entertainment lined up for you. Besides our own Frank Boulderbuster, Triambelong is lucky enough to have two other guests – magicians, in fact. They've only been here a few weeks, but they've already made themselves quite well-known. So, let's hear it for the blockbusting Beryl and the fantastic Fiery Flynn!'

Beryl and Fiery blew kisses to their audience, then bounded on to a stage which had been set up. At the back of the stage was a velvet curtain with 'Beryl and Fiery' stencilled on it in gold.'What a wonderful audience you are!' crooned Fiery Flynn, putting on a top hat and looking like a supreme showman. 'Do you all believe in magic?'

We all cried, 'Yes!', except for Raymond Goolie who called out something rude and got a wallop from Piggy for it.

'Well, you're about to see magic to perplex your peepers and boggle your brainboxes!' he cried. 'First, I need a lady volunteer!'

The Reverend Smog suggested Baron Herbert, who pinched him. It was Beryl Flynn who ended up volunteering.

'Now, I'd love to cut you in half!' said Fiery, in an evil voice.

For the first time that night Raymond Goolie looked interested.

'But that's too simple,' he added. 'Instead, I'm going to make you vanish altogether!'

'Oh help!' cried Beryl, pretending to be alarmed. 'I don't want to be disappeared!'

Fiery burst into fiendish laughter. Unfortunately, it made his false moustache fly off and land in the punch, where Frogwarble eyed it suspiciously. There was general laughter from the audience and more rude words from Raymond Goolie.

'Just get on with the act!' hissed Beryl.

'Er, right!' muttered Fiery, then put on his villainous voice again. 'Into the disappearing box you go!' he snarled, producing a large gold-painted box from behind the curtain. He took some care over where he placed it on the stage. Obligingly, Beryl climbed into the box. Fiery cackled, waved his bony arms and called out, 'Lo and behold!' There was a blinding flash and a puff of smoke. When the smoke had cleared he opened the door of the box to show that Beryl had indeed vanished. The audience applauded.

'Do not fear, ladies and gentlemen!' cried Fiery. 'The lady has not disappeared forever. She has simply entered another dimension – a dimension beyond the stars!'

'A dimension beneath the stage, you mean!' shouted Raymond Goolie.

'Young man,' smiled Fiery dangerously, 'what are you talking about?'

'She went down a trapdoor!'

'What a ridiculous suggestion! Why, she's beyond the stars at this very moment.'

'She's under your blooming feet!' giggled Raymond. Piggy silenced him by putting a bucket on his head. Fiery smiled thankfully at her.

'And now!' he bellowed. 'I shall bring the lady back by repeating the magic words, Lo and behold!'

There was another flash and another puff of smoke. Fiery opened the door again to reveal Beryl – or, at least, the top half of her. The rest was hidden beneath the stage.

'What happened?' he hissed, nervously.

'The lift's stuck!' muttered Beryl. 'Give us a hand, will you?'

With great embarrassment, Fiery pulled his wife out of the hole. The audience tried to do the polite thing and not laugh, but it was very difficult under the circumstances.

'Never mind about magic!' said Fiery, after the laughter had subsided. 'Beryl and I are here for quite a different reason.'

'That's right,' said Beryl, 'a different reason entirely.'

'You see, we are both scientists,' said Fiery. 'It was no accident that we arrived in Triambelong when the town was about to die.'

'No accident!' repeated Beryl.

'We make it our business to save towns,' explained Fiery, 'using science!'

'Science!' screeched Beryl.

'What we're telling you isn't just bulldust!' said Fiery.

'Bulldust!' repeated Beryl.

'Though we might seem like a couple of nuts to you.'

'Nuts to you!' cried Beryl, joyously.

'We've discovered how to save Triambelong, and we're going to show you our discovery tonight!'

'Come with us!' called Beryl. 'Let us take you to Project *Stargawk!*'

By this stage of the evening many people said that they were either too tired or too drunk to have anything to do with Project *Stargawk*. But Ernie Slag decided to play along with the Flynns. He let them borrow one of his covered lorries and invited anybody who wanted to find out about Project *Stargawk* to take a ride. Baron Herbert and the Reverend Smog, who were now arm in arm and singing raucous hymns, were the first to climb in. They were followed by Raymond Goolie.

'Come on, Frank!' laughed Piggy. 'This could be fun.'

I found Frogwarble happily staggering about on one of the trestle tables. Having drunk more punch than is healthy for an owl, she kept toppling out of the crown of my hat when I tried to put her there.

'Give her to me!' said Piggy. Carefully, she rested the drowsy owl in her handbag, which had somehow escaped Raymond Goolie's tomato sauce treatment.

The last to climb into the van was Ernie Slag, who closed the doors, then thumped on the wall next to the cabin. In reply, the Flynns drove off into the night.

Ten minutes later we piled out and found ourselves in the middle of the scrub.

'Stick close together and follow me!' ordered Fiery Flynn.

By torchlight, he led us through the scrub to a clearing.

'Wait a moment now!' said Flynn. He bent over and flicked a switch on a black box that rested on the ground. Instantly, the clearing was floodlit.

'There!' cried Beryl and Fiery Flynn. 'There is Project *Stargawk!*'

'Well, I'll be a blowfly's birthday present!' muttered Baron Herbert.

'Flipping hell!' added the Reverend Smog.

In the middle of the clearing stood a rocket made entirely of galvanised iron. On the nosecone was painted 'STARGAWK'.

'I can see you're wondering what this rocket is all about,' said Beryl. 'Tell them, Fiery!'

'It's our gateway to the universe!' marvelled Fiery.

'You pinched that lot from my factory!' said Ernie. 'There must be ten tonnes of top quality galvanised iron there!'

'Thanks to Beryl and me, you won't have to worry about iron anymore.'

'This rocket can reach other planets,' explained Beryl. 'We can collect every metal in the universe. Zinc, tin, copper, whatever you like! It runs on Fiery's special fuel, the most powerful thing ever invented.'

'The only powerful thing around here,' said Ernie, 'is your breath. You've obviously had too much of my black rum punch. Now, I suggest we all go home and stop behaving like a pack of silly galahs.'

'But we're launching the *Stargawk* tonight!' said Beryl.

'And I'm going up in it!' said Fiery.

The Reverend Smog went down on his knees, praying for Fiery Flynn to stop being 'a blinking, blooming, flaming idiot'.

'Don't worry about Fiery,' said Beryl. 'He'll be perfectly safe and quite comfy. I designed the inside of the rocket, you see.'

Proudly, she opened the rocket's iron door. Inside was a jumble of television parts and bits taken from an FJ Holden which the Women's Association had blown up two weeks before. In the middle was a couch, and cushions with views of Sydney Harbour on their covers. Three flying china ducks adorned the wall.

'I've used all the latest technology,' explained Beryl. 'To combat zero gravity, I stuck the ducks down with superglue.'

'I'VE USED ALL THE LATEST TECHNOLOGY,' EXPLAINED BERYL

Fiery Flynn climbed into the rocket, sat down and sticky-taped his backside to the couch.

'Ready for take-off, ground control!' he said.

Beryl, who was ground control, answered, 'All right, dearie. But you can't go yet. You need a number two.'

When it was suggested that Beryl climb in alongside Fiery, she shook her head vigorously.

'I can't do that! I'm ground control. I have to stay here to control the ground. Anyway, space flight brings on my arthritis.'

'And it gives her wind,' added Fiery.

Always one for practical jokes, Piggy volunteered to be Fiery's number two.

'That's the spirit!' Fiery grinned. 'Now your backside's bigger than mine, so you'd better use twice as much sticky-tape.'

After Piggy was taped in the two brave astronauts waved cheerio, then shut the rocket door.

'This is ground control!' Beryl yelled at the closed door. 'Commencing countdown. T-minus ten seconds.'

Piggy's muffled voice came from the rocket. 'Hang on a tick, ground control! Astronaut Piggy needs a wee.'

'The zero gravity potty is under the couch. Make sure you put the glad-wrap back on it. T-minus five seconds. Four, three, two, one, TAKE OFF!'

There was a brilliant flash at the rocket's base. Smoke billowed out. It was so bright we all had to turn away. When the smoke cleared the rocket had gone. And with it had gone Fiery Flynn and Piggy. Just then I remembered that Piggy had taken her handbag aboard. In it was Frogwarble, the first owl in space.

Though Beryl Flynn was delighted by the rocket's take-off, the rest of us weren't so happy.

'This is very peculiar!' said Ernie Slag. 'Triambelong

has never seen the like of it before.'

'There's nothing peculiar about space flight,' smiled Beryl Flynn. 'Fiery and I know what we're doing, so don't you worry about a thing.'

The Reverend Smog was still on his knees, praying for the unlikely astronauts. Raymond Goolie had found a welder's mask in the lorry. He was wearing the mask and moving about in slow motion, doing an impression of an astronaut. Ernie suggested we spent the night there.

'We can investigate this strange affair in the morning,' he said, 'but for the moment, let's climb into the lorry and get some sleep.'

THERE WAS A BRILLIANT FLASH AT THE ROCKET'S BASE

Some of us had headaches when we woke the next morning. Ernie Slag's black rum punch gave hangovers that were bigger than mountains and just as hard to get over.

'Holy blooming blazes!' moaned the Reverend Smog, as he got up off the lorry floor. 'My head feels as if it's been sat on by a flipping elephant.'

'Now, now, Smoggy!' muttered Baron Herbert. 'Today is Sunday so you'd better stop your swearing!'

Before the two old warmongers could have more words, there was a loud thumping on the lorry doors. This did not help people's headaches one bit.

'Who's making that racket?' yelled Ernie.

'It's me! Beryl Flynn! Something incredible has happened!'

We opened the door to see Beryl hopping around in excitement.

'Out you get!' she ordered. 'You'll soon see why I'm so excited!'

Ernie Slag, Baron Herbert, the Reverend Smog, Raymond Goolie and I piled out. We followed Beryl Flynn to the clearing, where a surprise awaited us. The galvanised-iron rocket had returned. There was some dew on the nosecone which sparkled in the morning sun.

'Isn't it wonderful?' laughed Beryl. 'Fiery has come back already! I bet the rocket is full of precious metal that he's plundered from other planets.'

'That's ridiculous!' snapped Ernie. 'How could a rocket travel to a planet and back in one night? It doesn't make sense!'

'My husband's fuel makes the *Stargawk* super-fast.'

'Speaking of your husband, are you quite sure he's in there?'

'Well, I haven't checked yet,' admitted Beryl, 'but of course he's there.'

Beryl sprayed the rocket with a flit-gun to 'decontaminate any space germs', then opened the door. Baron

Herbert held up Raymond Goolie so that he could peer inside.

'There's nothing here!' piped Raymond.

'Nothing?' gasped Beryl. 'What about the crew, Miss Ironpot and Fiery?'

'They've gone!'

'Gone? Of course they haven't gone! They're probably hiding in there somewhere. Are you sure they're not behind the couch?'

'The only thing here is a note,' said Raymond, picking up a neatly folded piece of paper from the couch.

Baron Herbert set the boy down again and asked for the note, which Raymond only handed over after being offered some money.

'Great green gob-stoppers!' yelped Baron Herbert. 'This note's in some strange alien code!'

The Reverend Smog snatched the note from him and pointed out that he had been trying to read it upside down. Putting on his sermon voice, Smog read the note to us.

Dear Earthlings,

This note is being written by Galvons from the planet Galvo, two million light-years from Earth. We have imprisoned the strange Earthlings that we discovered aboard this rocket. They tried to steal our precious metals, which is against Galvon law. If you want to see these Earthlings again you must do as we say. Before your sun sets you will fill the rocket with as many precious metals as possible. The rocket will then take off for Galvo. When we receive the precious metals we will return the Earthlings to you. This is a warning – since we have no television, we Galvons spend our time watching your every move. So don't try any tricks.

Love from,

the Galvons

'Aliens have kidnapped my husband!' shrieked Beryl Flynn.

'Aliens have kidnapped my kindergarten teacher!' giggled Raymond Goolie.

'And they've kidnapped my owl,' I added sadly.

'These Galvons sound dangerous,' said Ernie Slag. 'We'd better do exactly what they say. Mrs Flynn, please direct us back to Triambelong so we can have a town meeting.'

'Just a blinking moment!' said the Reverend Smog. 'You can't have a meeting today. It's Sunday! You've got to listen to my blooming sermon!'

'In that case, we'll have the meeting in the church of iron, *after* your sermon.'

'And you'd better not make it too long,' warned Baron Herbert, 'or I'll chuck you to Galvo myself!'

'Quiet, you grizzly great grunnion!' replied the Reverend Smog. 'If you dare come to my church wearing that disgusting dress, I'll make sure I give the most boring sermon that anyone ever heard!'

As the old enemies bickered we were driven back to Triambelong to spread the sad news.

Baron Herbert went to the church of iron wearing a sensible grey suit and tie, so the Reverend Smog cut his sermon short by leaving out a lot of the 'bloomings' and 'blinkings' and 'flamings' and 'flippings'. After his sermon he let Ernie Slag take his place at the pulpit. Ernie told the tragic tale of Project *Stargawk* and the kidnapping of Fiery Flynn, Piggy Ironpot and Frogwarble. Dynamite Doris from the Triambelong Country Women's Association stood up to make a statement after Ernie's speech. Being slightly deaf, she spoke very loudly.

'I'm a true blue Triambelong woman, and I think I can speak for all of us.'

'Of course you can,' said her best friend, Gelignite Joyce.

'And I say this,' Doris yelled. 'We're not going to be bossed around by a bunch of kidnapping garbos!'

'You nong, Doris!' said Baron Herbert. 'Mr Slag wasn't talking about garbos. *I'm* a garbo! Mr Slag was talking about *Galvons*.'

'Galvons?'

'They're aliens, you blinking waxy-eared sack of super-phosphate!' cursed the Reverend Smog. 'If you didn't spend so much time blowing up blooming cars, Doris, you'd be able to hear proper.'

'Sometimes it's good being a bit deaf,' said Doris smugly, 'especially during your sermons.'

'Listen, everybody!' I yelled. 'We haven't got time to argue! We have to collect all the gold, silver and platinum we can find, then load that rocket up before nightfall, or goodness knows what those Galvons might do to Fiery, Piggy and Frogwarble!'

'Hang on!' yelled Doris. 'I'm not going to give my favourite jewellery to those gherkins! We don't even know where they live!'

'They're Galvons,' I said patiently, 'and they live two million light-years away.'

'You mean, they're not even Australian?'

Ernie Slag suggested to Doris that this might be so.

'In that case, those rascals could be capable of anything! We'd best do what the note says. Girls, fetch all your jewellery then follow Mr Slag to the rocket!'

The members of the Triambelong Country Women's Association went about their work with military efficiency.

In the clearing, the people of Triambelong sadly loaded their precious rings, watches, brooches, silver cups and even gold-rimmed spectacles into the *Stargawk*.

'I'm very sorry about this,' said Beryl Flynn. 'My husband and I have been dabbling in space travel for years but this is the first time we've ever come across hostile aliens.'

'Never mind, Mrs Flynn!' yelled Dynamite Doris. 'You poor little pineapple! You must be so worried about your husband!'

Beryl tossed in her pair of gold gypsy earrings.

'Yes,' she nodded. 'I hope he's all right. Fiery and I are very close, you know. Very close indeed.'

There was something odd about the way Beryl said that. It sounded as if she knew something we didn't.

When the door of the rocket was closed we all stood back, waiting for the launch. Those of us who had already seen it take off warned the others about the glare.

'I don't understand how the rocket can take off,' said Ernie Slag, 'if there's nobody inside it.'

I tried to think of an answer. 'I suppose if the Galvons are powerful enough to see us from two million light-years away, they must know how to control the rocket.'

'You may be right,' sighed Ernie. 'I'm just a country bumpkin. All this space business is very new to me.'

Suddenly, smoke poured from the bottom of the rocket.

'Lo and behold!' cried Ernie.

I turned to him. 'Those were the magic words that Fiery used last night!'

'I suppose it's the smoke that made me think of them,' said Ernie.

By now, the smoke was so bright that everybody had to turn their heads away. There was Beryl Flynn. To my surprise, I noticed she was grinning. I remembered what she had said about how close she was to her husband. All at once I realised what was going on.

Something on the ground caught my eye. It was the

welding mask that Raymond Goolie had been wearing last night. I grabbed it and put it on. Since the smoked glass in a welding mask is supposed to cut down the glare of a blow-torch, I figured it would also let me see what was going on in the clearing. Sure enough, I could see the rocket's outline through the bright smoke. But it wasn't taking off for the stars. It was sinking quickly into the ground. It was on a grass platform which worked like a lift. Without a second thought I ran to the rocket and leapt on to the nosecone, grasping it as it disappeared below ground level. Another grass platform slid across over my head, covering the hole. To the Triambelong people gathered in the clearing, it must have looked as though the rocket had disappeared in a puff of smoke.

As I gripped the nosecone of the rocket, I found myself in an underground hollow. Below me was Fiery Flynn. Fortunately, he hadn't seen me. He was too eager to lay his hands on the wealth of jewellery inside his false space rocket. Rings, watches and brooches tumbled out as he opened the door. He picked them up and giggled softly.

'You must be a Galvon!' I cried. 'How do you do?'

Fiery Flynn dropped the jewels and looked up in alarm. His light-blue eyes widened as he saw me.

'Lo and behold!' he cried 'Frank Boulderbuster! How did you get here?'

'I took the lift!' I said.

Then, with a cry of 'Going down!', I leapt on to Fiery Flynn and gave him a Frank Boulderbuster crunch-punch. I won't tell you exactly what this is, but you can be sure that Fiery Flynn saw more stars than any other astronaut has seen before or since.

After dealing with Fiery, I heard a muffled cry. It came from a dark corner of the dug-out. There was poor Piggy, bound from head to foot. When I finally got the ropes off her, she had a lot to say.

'That rotten, shoddy little con man Flynn!' she shuddered. 'That lousy, light-fingered ferret! I thought he was going to keep me tied up here forever!'

There was a soft 'Boobook' sound. Poor Frogwarble was still in Piggy's handbag. I took her out and patted her head a few times to welcome her back, then placed her in the crown of my hat.

'Tell me, Piggy, how did Fiery Flynn manage to overpower a big strong woman like you? Did he use magic?'

'Of course he didn't! He knocked me out with this rock!'

Piggy handed me a piece of bright pink quartz. The place was full of other rocks like it. I remembered where I had seen rocks like that before – at Ballarat, Bendigo, Kalgoorlie and Hill End.

'Let's go up in the rocket!' I said.

'You must be joking!'

'Only to the next floor,' I explained. 'You see, I've got some very interesting news to tell the people of Triambelong.'

It surprised the crowd to see the space rocket *Stargawk* slowly rise out of the ground. But what really stunned them was when the door opened and Piggy and I stepped out, looking as cool as a couple of camels camped under a coolibah tree.

'I've seen some flipping funny things in my time,' said the Reverend Smog, 'but this takes the blinking biscuit!'

'Well, I'll be a bald bandicoot's big toe!' gasped Baron Herbert.

'What's going on here?' demanded Beryl Flynn.

'I'm afraid we've foiled your plan to rob the Triambelong people,' I announced. 'Fancy you thinking we'd believe your story about Galvons!'

Even though she knew she'd been caught, Beryl Flynn

laughed. 'I suppose it was a pretty stupid idea. Fiery said it would work.'

'It might have worked in Brisbane,' I said. 'It might even have worked in Sydney or Melbourne. But it could never have worked in a town as smart as Triambelong!'

'He's right, you know!' said Dynamite Doris.

'Of course he is!' said Gelignite Joyce.

'My blooming oath he is!' shouted the Reverend Smog. 'But what the blinking hell is he talking about?'

Piggy told the crowd the true story of the Flynns' false space rocket. Of course, the people were a bit angry but they weren't too hard on Beryl Flynn because she was really a very nice thief. Not at all stuck-up, like *some* thieves.

After Beryl had told her story, it was my turn to speak.

'It's funny how some people can't see what's under their noses,' I said to the crowd. 'For instance, what have I got here?'

I held up the piece of pink quartz that had given Piggy such a headache.

'A rock!' yelled Baron Herbert.

'Top of the blooming class!' muttered the Reverend Smog.

'But it's not just any rock,' I said slowly. 'It's gold-bearing rock. The Flynns were so busy setting up their rocket swindle, they never realised they'd stumbled upon a gold mine!'

'Gold?' cried Dynamite Doris.

'Gold!' laughed Ernie Slag.

'Gold! Gold! Gold!' screeched Piggy's kindergarten class.

'Blooming gold!' said the Reverend Smog.

And that was how the Triambelong gold rush began.

So the dying town of Triambelong was saved by two

crooks who planned a robbery that went wrong. Fiery and Beryl Flynn went to gaol, though I've heard that they escaped not long ago. Apparently they were putting on a show for their fellow prisoners when they both disappeared in a puff of bright smoke.

I left Triambelong the next day with the piece of gold-filled quartz in my pocket. It would be enough to buy us flour and jam for another few months.

As for the Galvons, they've only ever been sighted by the people of Triambelong and, until another town steals Ernie Slag's recipe for black rum punch, things are likely to remain that way.

'GRAB HOLD! I'LL PULL YOU OUT!'

The Bells of Banunga

I couldn't work out why Frogwarble was behaving so strangely. She refused to sit still in the crown of my hat and just kept hooting at the sky, as if she were counting the stars. The night sky over Banunga was as clear as I had ever seen. The Banunga Gardens looked blue in the moonlight. Up ahead, a pinprick of light winked on the ground. It looked as if one of the stars had fallen out of the sky and come to rest in the Gardens. I picked up the glimmering thing. It was a bell; a shining silver jingle-bell the size of a walnut. It didn't seem a lot of use to a swagman but I pocketed it and continued walking, looking for a nice leafy tree under which to spend the night.

Frogwarble fluttered off my hat and spiralled up to the stars. She was joined by another owl and they called to each other playfully.

Suddenly the ground disappeared from under me. Everything went cold and black. I had fallen into a lake, slimy with algae. As I bobbed out of the water I saw a white figure holding a hand out to me.

'Grab hold! I'll pull you out!'

Moments later I sat dripping by the lake. My rescuer

was a tall snowy-bearded bloke who seemed to be wearing white pyjamas.

'I'm glad you came along!' I shivered.

'You're the third one I've fished out this week,' he said. 'You must be a bell-ringer. Welcome to Banunga, the bell-ringing capital of Australia! I'm the Mayor, by the way. Nugget Shuttlebuck's the name.'

'I'm Frank Boulderbuster,' I said, shaking his hand, 'but I'm not a bell-ringer.'

'Then what are you doing in the Banunga Gardens at midnight? Have you lost something?'

I realised that Frogwarble had gone. 'As a matter of fact I have!'

Before I could continue, Nugget replied, 'What a shame! I've also lost something.' He brought his spectacled face close to mine. 'My jingle-bell,' he said. 'I've lost my jingle-bell.'

I took the little bell from my pocket. 'Would this be it?'

'You found it! I hope the water hasn't ruined its tone.' He jingled it in his ear. 'No, it's just as good as before. Well, Frank, I believe I owe you a favour!'

'Rescuing me was enough.'

He shook his head. 'I'm the Mayor, remember. Just tell me what you've lost and I'll replace it for you.'

When I explained that I had lost an owl, Nugget didn't look so confident.

'Owls are tricky birds,' he said. 'I have an idea, Frank. You can stay at my place for the night, then search for your owl in the morning. You'll have to sleep in the bungalow, though. My wife Ethel hates strangers.'

On the way to Nugget Shuttlebuck's house we passed through the main street of Banunga; a cluster of old-fashioned shops and a Town Hall with a belfry.

'You've arrived at a very exciting time,' said Nugget. 'This Saturday is the Banunga Bell Jubilee. I do hope you'll join in.'

The moonlight shone through the belfry on top of the Town Hall. I saw somebody up there.

'Who could that be?' I asked.

'So you can see it too?' said Nugget.

'Of course! There's somebody in the belfry tower.'

'I've seen it twice now,' Nugget whispered. 'It haunts the ancient Banunga bell, the bell we call the Cardinal. That's a phantom, Frank. I hoped you wouldn't find out about that.'

I woke up late the next morning in the Shuttlebucks' bungalow. From the window, I saw a woman hanging out the white clothes which Nugget had been wearing last night. She turned around and caught me staring at her unusual hair. It was purple.

'Awake at last!' she said, in a voice like sandpaper.

'You must be Mrs Shuttlebuck,' I said. 'Good morning. I'm...'

'I know who you are! You're the one who put muck all over Nugget's bell-ringing costume. Just look at that sleeve!'

The costume looked as clean as a priest's collar on Sunday morning but I thought it best to change the subject.

'I like your purple hair!' I said.

'It's lilac. Mr Pinkerton made it for me and he reckons it's lilac. He's a window-dresser so he ought to know.'

'Where is Nugget?' I asked.

'He has to work,' she replied. 'Not like some. He'll be at the Town Hall, organising the Bell Jubilee.' She tossed her purple curls. 'Blooming bells! A Mayor should have better things on his mind than bells!'

'What about the phantom?' I suggested.

She stiffened. 'That's enough talk about phantoms. This town is mad enough without bogeymen in the belfry.' Ethel Shuttlebuck picked up her washing basket. 'I suppose you can have some of the left-over porridge for breakfast. But don't expect me to like you as much as Nugget does. Just because you found his jingle-bell he thinks you're Christmas!'

The main street of Banunga was a busy place that morning. Cars with interstate number-plates were double-parked everywhere. Tourists who had come to see the Bell Jubilee jostled for postcards of the Cardinal, the big old bell in the Town Hall belfry. On every street corner bell-ringers filled the air with clings and clangs to advertise Saturday's big event.

I forgot about Frogwarble for the moment and decided to look at the shop windows. Strangely enough, the displays looked as miserable as could be. The window of a children's wear shop featured a beach scene with models of children digging in the sand. It should have been cheerful but it looked as if the children had just buried a cat. In the wedding shop next door, three dummy bridesmaids scowled as though someone had poisoned the wedding cake. There were no dummies in the window of the toyshop but somehow the toys looked mean. Teddybears and cuddly toys had fierce expressions and seemed ready to bite people. Humpty-Dumpty dolls resembled rotten eggs. Why did the windows look so dreadful?

In the window of the fashion shop, a sad old man dressed in black put fashionable clothes on some dummies. Ethel Shuttlebuck had mentioned a window-dresser called Mr Pinkerton. Was this the bloke who had made all the miserable window displays? At that moment he was trying to create a picnic scene. Four dummies were gathered around a picnic table while a tree containing some stuffed birds was propped up in the corner. It looked as though a party of ghouls were holding a seance in a graveyard, with vultures watching. Something in the hollow of the fake tree caught my eye. It was a little brown-and-white-speckled stuffed bird which looked familiar. I climbed into the window display.

'Where did you find that owl?' I demanded.

The sad little man looked up in surprise. 'Are you talking to me?' he asked.

'Yes, I'm talking to you, Mr Pinkerton! You've stolen my owl, haven't you?'

'WHERE DID YOU GET THAT OWL?' I DEMANDED

'I *am* Mr Pinkerton,' he said miserably, 'but I am guilty of no other crime.'

The little stuffed bird certainly looked like Frogwarble but Mr Pinkerton seemed to be telling the truth.

'How awful to be called a thief,' he said. 'In front of my children, too!' He pointed to each of the dummies. 'Meet Stephanie, Shorty, Bailey and Bo. Please don't stare at Bo. She's been very sensitive ever since she lost her leg.'

'Er... good-day,' I mumbled. 'I'm Frank. Frank Boulderbuster.'

'They look almost human, don't they?' marvelled Pinkerton. 'It's my job to fool people, you see. Plastic trees, fake animals, wigs – it's all make-believe.'

'If you'll all excuse me,' I said, 'I'd best go on looking for my owl.'

Pinkerton blocked my path. 'You'll never find your owl in this town. There are too many back streets; too many hidden nooks and crannies.'

'What I need is an aerial view,' I said. Then a brilliant idea hit me. 'I'll climb up to the belfry.'

'Not the belfry!' gasped Pinkerton, raising his delicate hands in shock.

'I'm not frightened by any tales about phantoms!' I said.

Pinkerton moaned, 'If you're determined to stir up the phantom by going to the belfry, I suppose I should go with you. A really horrible scare might cheer me up.'

After bowing to the crowd of window-shoppers who had watched our performance, we headed for the belfry.

The Cardinal

This is the cherished Cardinal bell of Banunga. It was made in 1280 and kept for six hundred years in a French monastery. According to tradition, the Cardinal must be rung only once every hundred years. If not, there will be a great flood, or possibly a great drought, or maybe just a cool change.

Nobody is quite sure. The Cardinal is now owned and loved by the people of Banunga. In the year 1880 the bell was rung for the first time on Australian soil and Banunga prospered. May those who ring it in the centuries to come never be plagued by great floods, great droughts or cool changes.

This was the plaque alongside the Cardinal. It was certainly a splendid bell, as tall as a person and as wide as a tractor tyre. It would have been interesting to look under it, but the bell was too close to the floor. Instead I leant on the rail of the belfry, looking out at the countryside.

'What a great view!' I said. 'Do many people come up here?'

Pinkerton shook his head and his hairpiece blew off, revealing thin grey locks underneath. He was much older than I had thought; at least seventy.

'It's always windy in Banunga!' he cursed, refitting his hairpiece.

In the Gardens at the top of the main street I could see brightly dressed bell-ringers practising.

'That's where I fell in last night.' I pointed to the lake. 'I wonder if Frogwarble could be on that island?'

'No chance of that,' Pinkerton replied flatly. 'I made it, I should know. It's artificial, you see. It always floats in the dead centre of the lake. Kids try to jump on to it from the lakeside, but they always miss and Mayor Shuttlebuck has to haul them out.'

'It looks so real!' I marvelled.

'Thank you. I built it for our very first bell festival fifty years ago. We have one every year, you know. This year it's time to ring the Cardinal again.'

'But what about the phantom?'

Before Pinkerton could answer, we heard footsteps. They were coming up the Town Hall stairs. We crouched behind the Cardinal, keeping an eye on the trapdoor we had climbed through to reach the belfry. From the trapdoor emerged a plump old woman. She was easily as old as Pinkerton, but dressed more colourfully in layer upon layer of silk scarves.

'Old Gloria!' cried Pinkerton, leaping out before the squat old woman. 'What are you doing up here, you horrible old troll?'

'Horrible old troll indeed!' Old Gloria snapped back. 'I am the gypsy of Banunga. I can read minds. I can tell fortunes. And I can squash your nose in if you don't look out.'

Before I had a chance to introduce myself, Old Gloria placed her wrinkly hands on the Cardinal and cried out in a sing-song voice, 'Phantom of the bell! If you hear me, give me a sign!'

'Push her off the tower, oh phantom!' suggested Pinkerton.

There was a sudden gust of wind. 'A sign! A sign!' Old Gloria chanted.

'Let's leave her alone,' Pinkerton whispered in my ear. 'Once Old Gloria starts chanting she keeps it up for hours, especially if she's been at the blackberry nip.'

'Let's stay!' I suggested.

'I can see a monastery!' she intoned, keeping one hand on the bell and putting the other to her lined forehead. 'It's a vision! A vision! This bell used to hang in a monastery in France! I see it clearly.'

'So do I,' muttered Pinkerton, 'on that plaque over there.'

'In the bell-tower a poor old hunchback is tugging the bell rope. Two monks are laughing at him, poor thing. He's all tangled up. The ropes are caught around his feet. He tries to struggle free but is lifted high into the air. The monks watch him dangling upside down. Oh no!'

I was getting very involved in the tale. 'What happens next?'

'The hunchback starts to swing himself towards the wall...'

'Yes?'

'He grabs hold of a brick sticking out but it crumbles away...'

'Yes?'

'He swings back upside-down and crashes into the Cardinal. It's ghastly! His head smashes right off! "Who's that?" one monk asks. The other replies, "I don't know, but his face rings a bell." '

Either Old Gloria was fond of telling horrible old jokes, or she had just worked out that a headless hunchback was haunting the Cardinal.

'This phantom character has got us all worried,' said Nugget Shuttlebuck, downing a glass of shandy. 'There was even talk in the council meeting today of not ringing the Cardinal on Saturday. We put it to the vote tomorrow. These are troubled times, Frank, troubled times.'

We were sitting by the window of the Bellbottom Inn. In spite of Nugget's talk of troubled times everyone in the pub seemed merry enough. A group of tough bell-ringers known as the barbells stood around knocking back drinks strong enough to eat through a fridge door.

'That's enough of my problems, Frank,' said Nugget. 'How was *your* day? Did you find your owl?'

I was distracted. 'Nugget! Can you see something moving in the belfry?'

Even in the darkness there was no mistaking the ghostly silhouette which hovered around the Cardinal. Either its head was bowed or... *it had no head at all!*

'That's the third time I've seen it!' gasped Nugget, his face white.

I put on my hat and made for the door.

'Frank, where are you going?' Nugget cried.

'To find a phantom! Anyone who's brave enough, follow me!'

The barbells huddled quietly in the corner. Nobody made a move. Finally, Nugget slammed down his drink.

'I can't let you go alone,' he said. 'You haven't bought your round yet.'

I slapped him on the back. 'This should be quite a night, Mayor!'

Nugget misheard me. 'A nightmare is exactly what it will be!' he muttered.

We stood alone in the belfry.

'What a shame! The phantom's gone!' puffed Nugget. The run up the stairs had been hard. 'And I was itching for a fight, too. Ah well, let's go back to the pub. I believe you owe me a shandy.'

'Hang on, Nugget!' I said. 'If we're going to catch this foul phantom we should search for clues.'

'Good idea! You stay here and look for clues while I go and buy more drinks...'

The words stuck in Nugget's throat. I soon saw what had knocked the wind out of him. A message had been daubed on the bell. It gleamed in the moonlight.

Whosoever rings this bell
Is doomed to burn and bake in hell

Yours,

The Phantom

The message was written in dark liquid which trickled down the bell's side. Shakily, I wiped it off and looked at the smear on my hands.

'It's blood!' gasped Nugget. 'Blood from the phantom's neck!'

We fled from the Town Hall to meet a crowd of people waiting on the steps. At the front stood Old Gloria with a bottle in her hand and a mangy black cat at her feet.

'What are you all doing here?' demanded Nugget.

'You can't hide the truth from us, Mayor Shuttlebuck!' cried the biggest barbell, who had the name Marvin O'Larrikin stitched on his singlet. 'Old Gloria has told us what's going on.'

Nugget gave Old Gloria an ugly look. 'What rubbish have you been telling them?'

Old Gloria waved her arms like a bad actress playing Shakespeare. 'I told them about the poor hunchback whose head was split open on the Cardinal. He's the phantom who haunts the belfry.'

'You've been at the blackberry nip again,' said Nugget. 'Hand over that bottle please.'

Old Gloria hugged it to herself. 'The bottle stays with me! Anyway, it's not blackberry nip, it's a potion to banish the phantom. It's an ancient blend of nettles, foxtail grass, Peruvian heliotrope and lino-polish.'

'Unless the phantom goes,' roared O'Larrikin, 'me and the boys are going on strike.'

A ghastly howling noise filled the air. Everyone was relieved to discover that it was only Old Gloria's mangy cat exercising its vocal chords. Old Gloria picked the creature up and stroked its scrawny neck.

'What is it Stinkwort?' she asked the cat. 'You hear the phantom approaching, do you? Oh, wise and true creature!'

Stinkwort howled again and bit Old Gloria on the ear.

'Filthy old fleabag!' she cursed, dropping the cat.

But something *was* approaching. From the direction of the Gardens came the sound of a galloping horse and the ringing of bells, getting steadily louder.

'It's the phantom!' cried O'Larrikin, the tattoos standing out like advertisements on his gooseflesh. 'All right, boys, let's leave Old Gloria to nobble the nasties on her own!'

'I DON'T FEAR YOU!' CHANTED OLD GLORIA

He tried to run but fear froze him to the spot. For galloping down the road towards us was a horse. And on its back, a caped rider with bells tied to his legs lurched forward in the saddle.

'Agent of darkness, you do not scare me!' chanted Old Gloria, bravely facing the horse and rider. She opened her bottle and sprinkled some potion in front of her. O'Larrikin made little whimpering noises as the mysterious figure on horseback rode closer and closer.

'Is it my imagination,' whispered Nugget, 'or does that rider have something missing?'

We could now make out the rider clearly as he jolted up and down in the saddle. He was dressed completely in red. His shoulders were uneven as if his back were badly hunched. And on top of those shoulders was... *nothing*.

'I don't fear you!' chanted Old Gloria. 'I will not budge!'

The red rider loomed over her terribly.

'Ooh heck!' she cried.

We scrambled up the Town Hall steps and cowered in the doorway as the horse and ghostly rider pounded off into the night. Soon all that could be heard was the distant, dying chime of bells. Thoughtfully, Old Gloria took a swig from her bottle.

'This could be trickier than I thought,' she said.

Ethel Shuttlebuck plonked a bowl of devilled kidneys in the middle of the dinner table. 'There's brains to follow,' she fumed. 'They're cold as death, of course.'

'I don't mind cold brains, love,' said Nugget.

Ethel tossed her purple curls. 'Those kidneys were the best in Banunga, the butcher told me. And those brains were from the brightest sheep. But you had to stay in the pub with Mr Boulderbuster, sinking shandies while your dinner spoiled!'

'Mum, I'm not hungry!' whined Shadrach, the Shuttlebucks' seven-year-old son. 'Can I watch a video instead?'

'You shouldn't sit in front of that television all the time!' said Nugget. 'It's bad for your eyes.'

Like his father, Shadrach wore thick glasses. 'Dad, you said I could watch videos tonight!'

'I'm sorry, Shadrach, but I forgot to pick them up from grandma's place. Anyway she hasn't finished with *War Demons of Hell* yet.'

'Really, Nugget!' growled Ethel. 'I thought you would at least remember Shadrach's videos.'

'I've had a lot on my mind,' said Nugget. 'These are troubled times.'

'Besides, we've been hunting for a headless phantom,' I said.

'What was that?' Shadrach piped up, suddenly interested. 'Did you really see a headless phantom?'

'It's nothing to get excited about,' said Nugget. 'As headless phantoms go, it was really quite ordinary.'

'Which video was that?' asked Shadrach.

'It was real life,' he explained.

'Oh, *that!*' Shadrach lost interest.

'Headless phantom indeed!' scoffed Ethel. 'I never heard a worse excuse for missing dinner! Next you'll be telling me there are bogeymen in the backyard.'

There was a tapping on the back door. It opened slowly and a cold gust of wind blew in. Just then, Mr Pinkerton entered. He was carrying something small, hairy and orange.

'Mr Pinkerton, you frightened the life out of us!' Ethel laughed nervously.

He waved the orange thing at her. 'I've brought you a little present, sweet Mrs Shuttlebuck!'

'My new wig! Oh thank you, Mr Pinkerton!'

'Not at all, you delightful macaroon. I made it myself from genuine horse-hair.'

'Where did you find an orange horse?' asked Nugget.

'He dyed it, you nong!' said Ethel, jamming the wig on her head. 'What do you think?'

'You look as if a ginger tomcat died on your head,' said Nugget.

'Gorgeous!' gushed Pinkerton. 'You look even more gorgeous than before.'

'Nugget, why can't you be a gentleman like Mr Pinkerton? At least offer him a beer.'

'No thank you,' Pinkerton smiled. 'I gave up drinking when I was twenty-one. Besides, I don't want to stagger home drunk when there's a headless phantom on the loose. Everyone in town is talking about it.'

Nugget frowned. 'Darn it, I was afraid that would happen! We might have to cancel the Jubilee after all.'

'I hope not!' said Pinkerton. 'You must ring the Cardinal. Don't be put off by silly threats.'

'What silly threats?' I asked.

'All that nonsense about burning and baking in hell.' he replied. 'Somebody told me it was written on the bell.'

Ethel smiled charmingly. 'Would you like a brain, Mr Pinkerton?'

'How nice! Just a headful, if you don't mind.'

'They're really fresh,' said Shadrach. 'Probably still thinking.'

Pinkerton decided not to have a brain after all. He turned to me and asked, 'Have you found your poor little owl yet?'

'She'll turn up eventually,' I replied.

'I hope so, Mr Boulderbuster!' he said. 'I really do hope so!'

With that, he disappeared into the windy Banunga night.

It was Friday and Frogwarble was still lost.

'Could you mention Frogwarble in the council meeting?' I asked Nugget, as we made our way to the Town Hall.
'This meeting could be tricky,' said Nugget.
The belfry cast its shadow over us. Next to the Town Hall steps rested an old bicycle with unmatching wheels.
'That's Old Gloria's bicycle,' said Nugget grimly, 'which means she'll be in the visitors' gallery stirring up trouble, as usual.'

The council chamber was an antique room with twelve seats surrounding a long table. Far above the chamber was the visitors' gallery with a balcony which ran the length of the front wall. As we entered the council chamber, Nugget and I had to duck to avoid a flying hammer.
'Councillor Duff!' yelled Nugget. 'You know the rules – *no throwing hammers!*'
'Sorry, Mayor!' stammered Councillor Duff. 'I was aiming at somebody in the visitors' gallery.'
The chamber was in a terrible state. Official documents lay everywhere and chairs were overturned.
'What a disgusting display!' said Nugget. 'This isn't Canberra, you know!'
'Old Gloria started it!' protested Councillor Duff.
Peering grimly over the gallery rail was Old Gloria, her mangy cat, Stinkwort, clasped to her big bosom.
'I never started anything,' she said innocently.
Councillor Duff's huge head turned red. 'You did so! You threw your ghastly cat at me!'
Nugget glared at Old Gloria. 'Is that true?'
'Of course not! Stinkwort was walking on the rail when she slipped and fell on to Councillor Duff's enormous head. He was cruel enough to swear at the poor little thing!'

Stinkwort bit her on the ear.

'Filthy old fleabag!' cursed Old Gloria, hurling Stinkwort back at Councillor Duff.

Nugget turned to me. 'Frank, could you please go up and stop Old Gloria flinging pets at the councillors?'

'With pleasure,' I replied, thinking it would be safer in the gallery than down there.

Nugget took his place at the end of the table.

'Now,' he said, 'we'll discuss the fire brigade's jumble sale.'

'Oh no you won't!' yelled Old Gloria.

The barbells clustered at her side. 'If you don't do something about the phantom now,' threatened Marvin O'Larrikin, 'me and the boys will jump up and down till the visitors' gallery falls on Councillor Duff's enormous head.'

'Oh, all right!' said Nugget. 'I recommend here and now that we go ahead with the Jubilee and ring the Cardinal bell tomorrow. Please cast your votes.'

Eight of the twelve councillors voted in favour.

Nugget smiled. 'Things will go ahead as planned!'

'But what about the phantom?' O'Larrikin demanded.

Stinkwort howled awfully.

'It's on its way!' gasped Old Gloria. 'The phantom is coming!'

Everybody listened. All that could be heard was Stinkwort's howling.

'Get that cat out of here!' ordered Nugget.

Then the phantom came. The jet-black horse with its headless rider burst in on the meeting. Hideous great hooves pounded the floor, councillors scurried in terror, O'Larrikin and his boys fainted. The red phantom leaned forward in the saddle, goading the horse on. All the while, we were deafened by the chime of the bells on the phantom's legs.

'I must get a closer look!' cried Old Gloria, dragging me by the arm. 'Come with me Mr Boulderbuster!'

As suddenly as they had appeared, the horse and rider bolted, leaving a flurry of dust and paper. Nugget Shuttlebuck, his spectacles broken, looked beaten.

'We won't ring the Cardinal after all,' he said, sadly. 'We must bow to the phantom's wishes.'

'Bulldust!' snapped Old Gloria. 'We can still defeat that nutless nightmare.'

'There's no time to natter!' I panted. 'Let's chase the phantom while we can.'

'We can go on my bicycle,' Old Gloria suggested, 'if you don't mind being dinked.'

Nugget ushered us to the door. 'I'd love to come with you but I'm blind as a bat without my spectacles.'

'Then look after Stinkwort,' said Old Gloria, thrusting her cat at Nugget. 'If she gives you any trouble, stick her in a piano.'

Dinking means two people riding on one bike. On Old Gloria's bone-shaker it was impossible to catch up with the horse and its rider.

'Can't you pedal any faster, Old Gloria?' I asked.

'I'm already busting my tights as it is!' she puffed. 'It's not easy, pedalling a passenger uphill.'

We finally reached the Banunga Gardens. It was a sunny afternoon and small groups of bell-ringers were practising on the lawn.

'Excuse me!' Old Gloria interrupted them. 'Have you seen a man on a horse? Crimson clothes and no head?'

The bell-ringers looked at us strangely and continued to clang away.

Standing on the lakeside, we gazed across at the floating island.

'I'm sure I saw something move amongst the bamboo!' Old Gloria whispered.

Suddenly we heard the horse's gallop, coming from

behind. We spun around to see the phantom charging us.

'Do you want to try your magic?' I asked Old Gloria.

'I have a better idea!' she said. 'Let's run!'

We parted. Seeing the lake, the horse stopped suddenly, causing the rider to tumble over its head and hit the water with a mighty splash. After a few seconds, only bubbles remained on the surface.

'It sank!' gasped Old Gloria. 'The phantom sank!'

Neighing, the horse galloped away.

I grabbed the bicycle. 'Come on!' I cried. 'When a horse loses its rider, it returns home. If we follow it we may find out who is behind this weird business.'

We screamed down the main street after the horse, passing the Town Hall, then skidding up a back alley. There were rows of storerooms. The horse's hoofprints led to a half-open storeroom door.

'After you!' smiled Old Gloria. 'There could be something nasty waiting in there.'

I wheeled the bicycle into the gloom. Old Gloria followed on tip-toe.

'Do you have a match?' she asked. 'This place is as dark as a warlock's whiskers.'

'I'll turn on the bicycle light!'

I switched it on. The yellow beam fell on something which made my blood run cold. On the floor was a grinning head.

Suddenly the place blazed with light and we saw that the head lying on the floor was the head of a shop dummy. There were dummies everywhere, standing in strange poses and grinning like ghouls. Alongside the light-switch stood Mr Pinkerton, waving a pistol at us.

'Mr Boulderbuster and Old Gloria!' he cackled. 'Now you know that I am the mastermind behind the phantom affair!'

'Mr Pinkerton!' Old Gloria gasped. 'You must be bonkers! Just wait till I tell Mayor Shuttlebuck about this!'

'You will tell nobody. If word gets out, I'll be ruined in this town!' He looked thoughtful for a moment. 'I have an idea! If you both leave Banunga right now and never return, I won't shoot you.'

'IF YOU BOTH LEAVE BANUNGA RIGHT NOW AND NEVER RETURN, I WON'T SHOOT YOU'

Old Gloria said, 'I've no intention of leaving Banunga, so you can stop this bally-hoo!'
'Then farewell!' cried Pinkerton.
The pistol clicked. Out popped a large pink flower.
'Stupid, isn't it?' moaned Pinkerton. 'I can't even shoot people properly!'
'There, there, Pinkie!' said Old Gloria, putting the flower in his buttonhole. 'Let's sit down and have a nice chat.'
Pinkerton nodded sadly. 'I know a spot where we can talk over a cup of tea.'
Old Gloria took a flask of blackberry nip from her many layers of clothes.
'I think we all need something a little stronger!' she said.

At the table sat Stephanie, Shorty, Bailey and poor one-legged Bo.
'We shouldn't be interrupted in this window display,' said Pinkerton, taking a seat next to Bo. Old Gloria poured out her blackberry nip.
'Here's to the Cardinal!' she said, raising her picnic cup.
'What a nong I've been!' said Pinkerton. 'All that effort to stop the Cardinal being rung.'
'But why?' I asked, scowling after finding a thorn in Old Gloria's blackberry nip. 'Once every hundred years can't hurt.'
Pinkerton put down his cup. 'Let me tell you a story about a bright young window-dresser. On his twenty-first birthday he goes out with a rowdy group of window-dressers and gets drunk.'
'Good idea,' mumbled Old Gloria, refilling her cup.
'The wicked window-dressers talk the birthday boy into a dare. They dare him to steal the clapper out of the

Cardinal, the bell that everyone in Banunga loves. The foolish boy scales the Town Hall fire escape and does the ghastly deed.' Pinkerton took a gulp of blackberry nip. 'That window-dresser is me.'

It sounded too incredible to be true. 'Do you mean, for the last fifty years, the Cardinal hasn't had a clapper?'

Pinkerton nodded. 'Nobody in Banunga ever knew, except me.'

'Then why don't you just replace it?'

'I was so drunk on that night, I can't remember where I hid it. It was somewhere in Banunga, but that's all I know.' Pinkerton's face was longer than a sword-swallower's sore throat. 'When they ring the Cardinal tomorrow and it makes no sound, the world will find out about my crime.'

'Things aren't that bad,' said Old Gloria. 'Even if people find out, they won't know who did it.'

'Oh yes they will!' said Pinkerton. 'That's the worst part of it all. On that night, fifty years ago, I not only removed the clapper, but I replaced it with something.' He shuddered at the memory. 'An unmentionable object. I've tried to remove it, but I've put on so much weight I can no longer reach under the bell. I've been up in the belfry these past few nights.'

That explained how the stories of the phantom had started. Outside the window little Shadrach Shuttlebuck was pressing his nose against the glass. To him, we must have looked like a giant television show.

'The first thing we have to do,' I said, 'is remove that unmentionable object from the Cardinal. I know just the person to do it!'

Shadrach Shuttlebuck gazed around the belfry.

'What a great place for a horror video!' he marvelled.

'Could you slip under the bell for us?' asked Pinkerton.

Shadrach's spectacles glinted orange in the light of the setting sun. 'That depends. What are you going to give me?'

Old Gloria turned to me. 'Do you have any money Frank?'

'I don't want your money!' said Shadrach. 'I want one of those wigs like mum's.'

'Curly or straight?' asked Pinkerton.

'Punk. All sticking up in the middle. And green.'

'Whatever you like!' said Pinkerton. 'Now, slip under the bell and close your eyes! The unmentionable object should not be seen by little boys.'

As soon as Shadrach crawled under the bell he burst out giggling.

'You've opened your eyes, you shameful boy!'

'Guess what I can see!' chuckled Shadrach.

'Just remove it please,' said Pinkerton.

We watched as Shadrach passed out the unmentionable object from under the bell.

It was a leg. It was poor Bo's left leg wearing a saucy red garter and a fishnet stocking. There was a little nest on the foot, and in the nest sat Frogwarble.

'What a strange creature!' Pinkerton exclaimed. 'Some people have the oddest pets!'

Shadrach picked up Frogwarble and patted her head. Sitting in the nest were three speckled eggs.

'So that's what you've been up to!' I said.

Pinkerton eyed the leg fondly. 'Poor old Bo will be so pleased to get this back! But first we should hide that nest out of harm's way in the Gardens. It's a perfect place for hiding things.'

Leaning on the belfry rail, I looked out towards the Gardens. The wind was growing colder as the sun was sinking.

'It's very odd,' I said. 'No matter how hard the wind blows in this town, that island always floats in the middle of the lake.'

'It always has,' said Pinkerton, 'ever since I put it there fifty years ago.'

'Mr Pinkerton,' I said, 'fifty years ago you had your twenty-first birthday.'

Old Gloria's eyes lit up. 'I think Mr Boulderbuster has found out where the Cardinal's clapper is!' she laughed.

All I needed was the help of Marvin O'Larrikin to return the clapper to its rightful owner.

'No blooming fear!' yelled Marvin O'Larrikin. 'I'm not diving into that freezing cold lake.'

'But someone has to pull the phantom out,' said Old Gloria, 'and everyone knows you're the bravest, strongest man in Banunga.'

O'Larrikin swelled with pride. 'What's in it for me?' he asked.

'How would you like a nice punk wig?' Pinkerton suggested.

I had a better idea. 'If you pull out the phantom,' I bargained, 'you can have the bells on its legs.'

'But those bells belong to me!' Pinkerton cried.

Old Gloria nudged Pinkerton. 'What was that you said?'

'Never mind,' he grumbled.

By the time we reached the Gardens, night had fallen. I placed Frogwarble's nest in the fork of a ghost-gum. There was a huge splash as Marvin O'Larrikin dived into the lake. Moments later, he bobbed up, covered in weed.

'Did you find it?' asked Pinkerton.

'Not yet!' spluttered O'Larrikin. 'I must be a lunatic to do this!'

He took a large gulp of air then duck-dived. The three of us stood watching the moon's reflection in the water.

'I've found the phantom!' O'Larrikin cried, bobbing up for the third time. 'It's tangled in some sort of chain.'

'That's the anchor chain!' cried Pinkerton excitedly.

'Show us how strong you are and pull up the anchor!' Old Gloria said.

O'Larrikin dived under, then returned with a roar. He heaved a big oblong piece of iron on to the lakeside and the headless body of the phantom rose to the surface. O'Larrikin had removed the brass bells from it.

'Just think, the whole of Banunga was terrified by this!' panted O'Larrikin, tossing the body on to the bank. Lying on the grass, it looked no more frightening than a shop dummy, for that was what it was; Mr Pinkerton's home-made phantom.

'Just wait till I show these bells to the boys!' smiled O'Larrikin. 'And wait till I explain how I got them!'

Putting on his singlet and pants, he raced off into the night, ringing the bells as loudly as he could.

'I hope young Shadrach is waiting for us!' grunted Pinkerton as we hauled the huge iron weight up the Town Hall staircase. 'He's the only one small enough to slip under and replace the clapper.'

'Phew!' gasped Old Gloria. 'How the heck did you shift this thing when you were twenty-one?'

'I had muscles in those days!' said Pinkerton. 'I used to be a real iron-man.'

'Well, I can't carry it any more!' Old Gloria dropped the weight. Pinkerton stumbled. Now I was the only one holding the clapper and it was beginning to slip back down the stairs. I held fast. The muscles in my arms bulged. Taking a deep breath, I heaved it on to my shoulders.

'Good heavens!' cried Old Gloria.

'Amazing!' Pinkerton breathed. 'But if you're so strong, why didn't you fish it out of the lake yourself?'

'I've already been in that lake,' I said, 'and once is enough!'

I eased the enormous load from my shoulders on to the floorboards of the belfry.

'Where's my wig?' demanded Shadrach.

'You'll get your wig,' snapped Pinkerton, '*after* you've replaced the clapper.'

'I can't lift that thing! I'm not Superman!'

Pinkerton looked crestfallen. 'How are we going to attach the clapper?'

Quickly, I shinned up the bell-housing until I was standing astride the Cardinal. There was a big iron ring at its top. Gripping a sturdy wooden beam overhead, I tucked my feet into the ring, then tried to lift the bell.

'Come down, Mr Boulderbuster, before you injure yourself!' yelled Pinkerton.

'Let him try!' said Old Gloria. 'You saw what he did before!'

I strained till I saw shooting stars. The bell creaked slowly upwards.

Carrying the clapper, Old Gloria, Pinkerton and Shadrach struggled under the bell. I had a nasty feeling I might drop it and leave them trapped, but my strength held out. There was a loud cheer of victory.

'We're all clear now,' said Pinkerton. 'You can lower the Cardinal!'

I let it down gradually.

'Well done!' Pinkerton said joyfully. 'I haven't felt so happy in fifty years!'

'Wait till I tell everyone about this!' said Shadrach.

'If you tell anybody at all,' warned Pinkerton, 'I'll grind you up till you look like this!'

He squeezed his fist and some red sticky liquid dripped out.

'Blood!' whispered Shadrach, impressed. 'Just like in the videos! Don't worry, Mr Pinkerton, I won't tell!'

Pinkerton opened his hand to reveal a tube of stage blood – the sort used in plays and films. With the fake blood, he daubed on the bell:

Don't mind what I wrote last night,
Ring this bell with all your might!

Fond regards,

The Phantom

The Cardinal's deep, rich tone echoed beautifully through the town of Banunga. In the Gardens people tossed their hats into the air.

'Did you ever hear such a wonderful sound?' said Nugget Shuttlebuck, dressed in his best bell-ringing costume.

'The French certainly know how to make their bells,' I said.

Marvin O'Larrikin, sweating after a ringing session with the barbells, rolled up to us.

'Lovely Jubilee, Mayor!' he said. 'I've just been telling the boys about how brave I was last night!'

'He knocked out the phantom!' one of the barbells cried in admiration.

'That's right boys!' O'Larrikin beamed. 'I punched him right in the nose!'

Old Gloria scuttled up and slapped him with her cat, Stinkwort. 'You great fibber,' she scolded. 'How could you punch it in the nose when it didn't even have a head?'

O'Larrikin blushed and crept away.

'We know the real story behind the phantom, don't we!' smiled Old Gloria, the smell of blackberries on her breath.

'That's right!' I nodded. 'It's a secret between you, me, Mr Pinkerton and Shadrach.'

Shadrach strutted by, his hair all green and spiky.

'Mr Pinkerton didn't give me the wig,' he explained, 'so I did it for real. Looks great, doesn't it?'

Not far away, Ethel Shuttlebuck was arguing with Mr Pinkerton.

'I thought you were such a gentleman,' she said, 'but you've been giving Shadrach terrible ideas! Just look at him – a grotty little punk!'

'Don't worry, dear Mrs Shuttlebuck,' Pinkerton said gently. 'Lots of people wear their hair like that these days!'

He lifted off his dowdy black hairpiece. Beneath it, his real hair stuck up all spiky and pink in the Saturday morning sunshine.

'I feel like a different man!' he grinned.

I whispered to Old Gloria. 'I don't much like Mr Pinkerton's new hairstyle.'

She laughed, 'You should talk! Have you seen how silly *you* look?' She pointed at my hat.

I suppose I might have looked a little silly. In the crown of my hat was Frogwarble's nest, a little mess of feathers and twigs. She hooted contentedly as she sat on her eggs. Until they hatched, she would have to stay there.

'Come on, Frank!' cried Nugget. 'Join in the Jubilee!'

Old Gloria and I joined the crowd as the Cardinal rang. It was going to be a very good century.

'BEAUTIFUL PUMPKINS!' YELLED A HUGE FARMER AT HIS STALL

The Night of the Pumpkin-Heads

There is nothing worse than a busted boot in the middle of a Victorian winter. The sludge leaks through to your toes and keeps them as cold as ice. Of course Frogwarble didn't mind the winter so much. Owls have nice warm feathers to fight off the chill. Besides, she was asleep in the crown of my hat, far from the icy ground.

I was walking around the Nar Nar Goon market, trying to find a boot repairer who didn't charge too much.

'Beautiful pumpkins!' yelled a huge farmer at his stall. 'Butternuts! Crown princes! Queensland blues! Beautiful pumpkins!'

'Don't buy those pumpkins!' yelled a smaller farmer at the opposite stall. 'They're full of fungus! Buy my potatoes instead – beautiful King Edward potatoes, lovely for fish and chips!'

'You'd be bonkers to buy those potatoes!' cried the first farmer. 'They've got so many worms, the chips crawl all over your plate!'

The two farmers strode out from behind their stalls and were about to clobber each other when a bloke pedalling a strange-looking tricycle rode up between them.

'Ice-cream, anyone?' the bloke asked. He looked a weird sight. His tricycle had two wheels in front and one behind. Between the two wheels was a large box with 'BLIGHTER'S DELIGHTS' painted on the side. 'Care for an ice-cream, sir? Flavour of the day is coolibah coconut.'

It seemed silly to sell ice-cream on a cold day like this, but the salesman had plenty of customers. Young and old flocked to sample the ice-cream, which looked like dollops of brightly coloured mush. Since I couldn't afford a Blighter's Delight, I went trudging on, stomping my feet every now and then to keep them warm. There were plenty of boot repairers but they all charged at least five dollars just to whack some leather on your heels. Five dollars was too much. At that moment all I had to my name was the blanket on my back, a small bag of flour, a half-empty bottle of jam and sixty-seven cents in small change. I was about to leave the market when one of the sideshows caught my eye. It was a big canvas tent with a sign painted on the outside.

'Who dares fight the amazing Zoola Hubbard?
Twenty dollars will be awarded to anyone who can defeat this wonderwoman of steel.
Free first aid will be given to the losers.'

On a platform outside the tent stood the amazing Zoola Hubbard. She was a bulky woman, dressed in the sort of clothes that jockeys wear; white breeches and a satin shirt.

'Reckon you can beat me, mister?' she said.

I sized her up. She looked tough but not unbeatable. Sensibly, she wore a rubber skullcap so that her hair was out of harm's way. On the cap was a picture of a rat.

'How much will it cost me to fight you?' I asked.

'It won't cost you a cent if you beat me,' she replied.

'And if I don't?'

'It'll cost you ten bucks. But we do give you a free ambulance ride.'

I had fought with boxing ghosts, roughnecks and crocodiles. Could I beat the amazing Zoola Hubbard?

'I'll take you on,' I said. 'Just give me half an hour to warm myself up.'

Zoola Hubbard grinned triumphantly. 'He's going to fight me! The swaggie's going to fight me!'

The word spread like a mouse plague.

'That swaggie must be off his rocker!' I heard someone cry.

The salesman on the ice-cream tricycle quickly recognised an opportunity to sell more ice-cream. He parked outside the tent, calling, 'Ice-cream! Ice-cream! Buy a Blighter's Delight and enjoy the fight!'

I had half an hour to warm myself up. My breath came out in large, misty clouds as I jogged up and down the stalls.

'You don't know what you've let yourself in for!' laughed the pumpkin farmer. 'Zoola Hubbard is a hurricane on legs!'

I grabbed four of his enormous blue pumpkins.

'Put those back!' he said, turning fierce.

'Just watch this!' I told him, taking off my hat and placing it on the trestle table. A crowd gathered. Even Frogwarble woke up to watch.

Slowly, I tossed the mighty pumpkins into the air then caught them.

'All right, so you can toss a few pumpkins,' said the pumpkin farmer. 'So what? Zoola can turn over a tractor!'

'But can she do this?' I asked.

Suddenly I went into my famous pumpkin-juggling routine, which has made me a legend in most pumpkin-growing countries. I tossed them from hand to hand, over my head, then under my legs. Round and round the four pumpkins flew till they looked like nothing but a blue blur. Out of the corner of my eye I saw the astonished pumpkin farmer's mouth hanging open so wide I could have tossed one of the pumpkins down his throat without it even touching the sides.

'What wonderful arms you have!' marvelled the pumpkin farmer. 'Listen, mate, if ever you want a job picking pumpkins, just come to me. I could use a bloke with arms like that!'

My half-hour warm-up was nearly over.

'Place your bets!' cried the potato farmer who, it seemed, was also a bookie. 'Ten to one against the swaggie!'

The bookie obviously thought I had no chance of winning. But after my brilliant juggling display a lot of people were putting their money on me. Stupidly, the bookie didn't lower the odds. If I ended up winning the fight with Zoola Hubbard this bookie would have a lot of money to pay out.

'Good luck, swaggie!' said the pumpkin farmer. 'I hope my wife doesn't hit you too hard!'

'Your wife?' I gasped.

'Yeah,' he said, extending his enormous hand. 'I'm married to Zoola. Arnold Hubbard's my name. Take it from me, swaggie. You've got as much chance as a potato grub in a fish and chip shop.'

I took off my coat and blanket, then pranced around in my corner of the ring, punching the air. Zoola Hubbard stood magnificently in the opposite corner, her husband Arnold fussing over her.

Though it was freezing cold outside, the atmosphere in the tent was warm and smoky. It seemed as though the entire population of Nar Nar Goon had gathered to watch the big fight.

The bell rang.

Zoola and I circled each other, glaring menacingly. I opened with an excellent right hook. In a flash, Zoola shot out her right hand, chopped me on the neck, grabbed the front of my belt with her left hand, then yanked. Before I knew what had hit me, I was lying on the floor. There were peals of laughter from the audience. So this was why Zoola Hubbard was so amazing! She used the oriental art of ju-jitsu! Two could play at that game, I thought. Scrambling to my feet, I adopted the pose of a master of koo-wee-rup, the ancient martial art which I had learnt as a boy. Koo-wee-rup is much more powerful than ju-jitsu. Howling like a cat, I brought down my hand in a koo-wee-rup chop. Zoola stopped my chop, clamped a double wristlock on me and kicked my right foot. I ended up on the floor again. People cheered this time.

'Give up, swaggie!' yelled the bookie.

Since koo-wee-rup didn't work, I tried the ancient art of masi-fugu-sun. I closed my eyes, then thought of my body as a giant tractor tyre – rubbery and roly-poly.

I TRIED THE ANCIENT ART OF MASI-FUGU-SUN

Zoola gave me a sharp belly-jab. To my delight and her surprise, her hand bounced harmlessly off me. My masi-fugu-sun was working! Howling, Zoola ran at me and tried to head-butt me, but my rubbery belly just made her bounce back into her corner. Every time she tried to throttle me, I simply bounced her away. Before long the amazing Zoola Hubbard was beginning to tire. The crowd looked astounded. The bookie, thinking about all the money he would have to pay out, turned a nasty green.

I was just about to finish with Zoola when I felt a brain-boggling knock on the back of my cranium. It wasn't Zoola, I was sure of that. Just before I passed out, I heard Arnold Hubbard yell, 'Some rotten mongrel's clocked him with a potato!'

I woke up with a headache the size of the South Pole. I was sitting between Zoola and Arnold Hubbard in the cabin of a truck. Arnold had two little Hubbards sitting on his enormous knees. Zoola was at the wheel.

'Glad to have you back with us!' said Zoola. 'We were afraid that spud might have knocked you out for days.'

'It takes more than a spud to finish off Frank Boulderbuster!' I replied.

'So that's your name!' smiled Arnold. 'Butternut, Windsor, say hello to Mr Boulderbuster. He's a friend.'

The identical twin boys on his lap said hello. They looked exactly like miniature versions of Arnold. When I went to lift my hat to the boys I received a rude shock.

'Hey!' I cried. 'Where's Frogwarble?'

'If you mean your owl,' said Zoola, swerving to avoid a Blighter's Delight tricycle, 'then take a look behind you!'

There was Frogwarble, sound asleep on a ledge behind the seat. She looked a lot fatter than usual.

'That owl's a blooming nuisance!' said Arnold. 'When we left it alone at the market stall it ate four-dozen pumpkin seeds – almost half a crop of Queensland blues.'

Frogwarble hiccuped contentedly.

'I'm sorry,' I said. 'She usually eats flies.'

'No need to apologise, Frank,' said Arnold. 'You're part of the Hubbard family now.'

Zoola nudged me with her massive arm. 'I took a shine to you as soon as you started to clobber me.' She smiled. 'Stay with us for a few days, Frank.'

'Well...'

'You can help with the pumpkin harvest!' said Arnold. 'You'll like my pumpkins. And Butternut and Windsor will mend your boots for you. What do you say?'

I decided to take up the invitation. And that was when Butternut and Windsor started calling me Uncle Frank.

The truck sped up the driveway and skidded to a halt. The Hubbard pumpkin farm was small but tidy. There was a whole paddock of huge Queensland blue pumpkins ready for picking, and alongside it was another paddock which was empty.

'I'll plant new seedlings there in October,' explained Arnold, 'and next year I'll have pumpkins so big that even *you* won't be able to lift them.'

The sun peeped out weakly from behind a cloud. It shone on a large silver building which stood not far from the Hubbards' property. On its side was painted 'THE HOME OF BLIGHTER'S DELIGHTS'. Behind a high wire fence, seven ice-cream tricycles were parked. It looked ugly but Arnold didn't seem to mind.

'They never give us any trouble,' he said.

'And we get lots of free ice-cream,' said Butternut.

'If only our other neighbours could be so well-behaved!' said Zoola wistfully. 'But you don't want to know about them, Frank. Come inside and we'll stuff you with pumpkin pie. And there are enough dead flies on the window sill to keep your owl fed till Christmas.'

Just then, Arnold let out a blood-curdling yell. His face went red with anger. Too furious to speak, he pointed at the pumpkin patch. By the patch was an enormous compost heap which was being raided by a shady-looking trespasser.

'Tito Graffito!' he choked. 'Tito Graffito is nicking our compost heap!'

The whole Hubbard family, howling like Tasmanian devils, took hold of pitchforks and charged. Fortunately, they stopped just before puncturing Tito Graffito, who must have felt like the last cocktail frankfurter at a birthday party. He dropped the stinking compost at his feet.

'Don't stab me!' he begged. 'I was only admiring your compost heap!'

Arnold growled, 'You know perfectly well that heap is the pride of the Hubbard family. It took us years of loving work, piles of straw, manure and potato peelings.'

'Potato peelings which you stole from *me*!' returned Tito.

Butternut waved his pitchfork. 'You're trying to sabotage our pumpkins by making off with our compost!'

I butted in. 'Aren't you the bookie who tossed that potato at my cranium?'

'That's him all right,' said Zoola. 'He's the worst bookie in the business. He figured the only way to stop you winning the fight was to sock you with a spud.'

'You need to be taught a lesson, Mr Graffito!' I said.

Using the ancient art of masi-fugu-sun to rubberise my body, I sprang towards Tito and sent him flying over the barbed-wire fence back into his own messy paddock.

'That was fantastic, Uncle Frank!' cried Butternut.

'He won't try stealing our compost heap again!' added Windsor.

As we wandered up to the house, we were approached by a curious couple riding a two-seater ice-cream tricycle.

'Miss Blighter! Miss Blighter!' cried the twins, running to meet these newcomers. Miss Blighter, a well-dressed and handsome lady, waved from the seat of the tricycle.

'Park here, Doggo!' she ordered the small, weedy bloke who held the handlebars. I recognised Doggo as the ice-cream seller at the market.

'Do you have any free ice-cream for us today?' asked Butternut.

'Of course!' Miss Blighter smiled. 'Doggo, give each of the boys an ice-cream!'

From the box, Doggo produced two enormous brown ice-creams which he gave to the twins.

'You spoil those boys!' said Zoola.

'I always like to be nice to neighbours,' Miss Blighter said. 'Doggo, give Mrs Hubbard a blue heaven on a stick.'

'Not for me, thanks!' said Zoola. 'I'll be too flabby to fight. I almost got beaten today by Frank Boulderbuster here.'

'You must be quite a toughie!' Miss Blighter said to me. 'How would you like to work in my factory?'

'Thanks, Miss Blighter, but it seems I'm working for the Hubbards at the moment.'

Miss Blighter looked at me in disappointment. 'Well, when you get tired of pumpkins, come and see me. My factory's doing so well, we could pay you good money. We'll have to expand soon.'

'Now, now, Miss Blighter!' said Arnold. 'Stop trying to take our new family member away from us!'

Miss Blighter gave a thin smile. 'Wouldn't dream of it! Well, it's been nice meeting you, Mr Boulderbuster. I'm sure you'll get along well with the Hubbards.' She frowned at her underling. 'Doggo, drive me back to the factory!'

Before she had a chance to leave, a huge dollop of something white fell from the sky and splatted across her pin-striped jacket. For the first time that day Doggo smiled.

'I reckon you've been bombarded by a flying emu!' he giggled.

'Don't just stand there, Doggo! Get this muck off me!'

I looked up in the sky for a glimpse of the amazing bird that had done the dirty deed. There was another hail of warm white gunge.

'It's mashed potato!' cried Arnold. 'That ghastly Tito is launching mashed potato at us!'

Standing at the barbed-wire fence were Tito Graffito and his twin daughters. They cackled gleefully as they fired globs of mashed potato from a home-made giant catapult – an elastic harness fixed between two fence posts.

'Well done, Pommy and Terri!' said Tito, as the girls stretched back the harness as far as they could. 'We'll aim for that horrible Zoola this time.'

Pommy and Terri let go of the harness. Like a guided missile, the glob of mash landed right on Zoola's head. Luckily, she was still wearing her rubber skullcap. But some of the mash splattered onto her shiny satin shirt and breeches.

'This means war!' she bellowed. Like a squadron of fighter planes, the Hubbards took off in pursuit of the Graffitos. I was about to join the skirmish but Miss Blighter held me back.

'Take my advice Mr Boulderbuster!' she said. 'Don't get caught up in the family feud between the Graffitos and the Hubbards. They've been bitter enemies for years.'

'But I've got to stand by the Hubbards,' I said. 'Why, the twins have even started calling me Uncle Frank!'

'Then you're in worse trouble than you think!' said Miss Blighter. 'Drive on, Doggo!'

Frogwarble and I slept soundly in the pumpkin shed that night. There were no spare beds in the house but the straw in the shed suited me fine. At breakfast Windsor and Butternut were moaning about having to go to school.

'Why can't we stay home with Uncle Frank and get the Graffito girls?' whined Butternut. 'I want to pay back that Terri for putting mash in our gumboots.'

'Speaking of boots,' said Arnold, chomping on a big piece of pumpkin pie, 'when are you going to fix Uncle Frank's boots?'

'Let us stay home and do it!' suggested Windsor.

'If you don't go to school,' warned Zoola, 'you'll end up as stupid as the Graffitos.'

This frightened Butternut and Windsor so they collected their schoolbags and walked out the back door. Moments later they cried out in surprise.

'The compost heap has gone!'

We raced outside and saw that the boys were right. Not a whiff remained of the great creation. Tito Graffito, wearing a head bandage from yesterday's scuffle, leered over the barbed-wire fence.

'Compost heap gone walkabout?' he said.

'Of all the low tricks!' spat Arnold. 'Where have you put it, you potato-headed scrounger?'

'We haven't touched your stinky, scrappy skyscraper!' said Tito. 'Your problem is, you've got compost on the brain!'

'And you've got compost *for* a brain!' replied Zoola. 'We'll get even with you, Tito! Just you wait!'

After the boys left for school, Arnold and I spent the morning cutting the pumpkins from their shrivelled vines. We loaded the massive Queensland blues on to the truck, then drove to a nearby market. Frogwarble came along for the ride, keeping an eye out for more pumpkin seeds to gobble.

By the end of the day, all our pumpkins were sold (or 'sent to good homes' as Arnold put it). When we arrived back at the farm, Zoola was hanging out some washing. Most of it consisted of her immaculate fighting clothes – multi-coloured satins and snow-white breeches.

'I have some wonderful news!' she told us. 'Our compost heap is back again!'

Sure enough, there stood the heap at the end of the pumpkin patch. But somehow, the heap looked different. Not bigger or smaller, just different.

'So, Tito brought it back!' said Arnold.

'I'm not sure about that,' said Zoola. 'I've been at jujitsu class for most of the day. When I got home, there it was.' She looked suddenly serious. 'Does it look a bit... peculiar to you?'

'You'll think I'm crazy,' said Arnold, 'but I reckon that compost heap looks *mean*.'

Arnold was right. The compost heap *did* look mean.

Frogwarble downed a saucer of flies while Arnold and I ate our pumpkin pie for afternoon tea.

'It could be maggots!' suggested Arnold.

I looked at the pie in my hand. 'Tastes all right to me!' I said.

'I wasn't talking about the pie. I was talking about the compost heap. Maybe maggots carried it away and brought it back?'

There was a scream from outside. We dashed out to find Zoola lying on the ground with bits of muck all over her. As we helped her to her feet we were almost knocked out by a terrible pong.

'The... the... compost heap!' stammered Zoola. 'It got me from behind! It was moving!'

'What are you talking about!' laughed Arnold. 'It couldn't have been the compost heap! See, it's still at the bottom of the...'

Arnold went pale. I looked at the pumpkin patch and saw that the compost heap had gone again.

'Of course it was the compost heap!' stormed Zoola. 'What else could leave such a terrible stink? And the filthy thing's made off with the washing line! All my best satins were on it!'

'Then why didn't you use your ju-jitsu to stop it?'

'Arnold, that heap is bigger than a goal post! Anyway, how do I put an armlock on something without arms?'

Zoola was getting worked up. Arnold suggested that she have a cup of tea while we hunted the mobile heap. But it was nowhere to be seen.

Miss Blighter and Doggo appeared, on foot this time, with a box of ice-creams for Butternut and Windsor. Arnold accepted them without thanks.

'Arnold's had a terrible shock,' I explained to Miss Blighter. 'You haven't seen his runaway compost heap, have you?'

'I want to complain to you about that!' said Miss Blighter. 'Doggo, tell them what you saw!'

Doggo shuffled forward. 'Well, I was adding the pink colouring to a batch of rhubarb ripple when I thought I heard something creeping up on me. I felt an icy chill down my spine as if someone had dropped an ice-cream down my shirt.'

'Just stick to the facts, Doggo!' snapped Miss Blighter.

'When I turned there was this huge compost monster advancing on me. I yelled to the foreman and together we tried to fight the hideous thing. But I was bowled over and the foreman was knocked into the rhubarb ripple. It was awful! The colour was ruined.'

'In future, Mr Hubbard, please keep your compost heap under control!' said Miss Blighter. 'Good-bye for now. Come along, Doggo!'

Miss Blighter and Doggo sauntered back to the factory, where six ice-cream tricycles gleamed in the afternoon sunlight.

That evening the Hubbard family gathered at the fireside. Zoola practised her ju-jitsu moves while Arnold and I discussed the compost heap with the boys.

'There's something strange going on around here!' said Arnold. 'I've never known a compost heap to turn vicious before.'

'Maybe it's full of pumpkin fungus?' suggested Butternut. 'You know how nasty pumpkin fungus is!'

'Yes but fungus doesn't move things around, does it?' reasoned Windsor. 'You don't see mouldy pumpkins rolling about clobbering people!'

'If you ask me,' said Zoola, 'those Graffitos are behind this. They're all as foul as a chookhouse floor.'

There was an almighty crash. Broken glass fell on to the loungeroom carpet and cold air blew in, filling the room with compost heap stink. Frogwarble hooted and fluttered wildly around. We pressed against the wall and looked out of the window. A flash of lightning lit up the enormous compost heap which stood outside. Zoola's clothes hanging down made it look like a nightmarish Christmas tree.

'You... you don't scare us!' cried Zoola.

The wind blew colder. It brought with it the chilling voice of the compost heap.

'My heart is cold and mouldy!' it hissed. 'My only wish is to terrify! If you're not frightened now you soon will be!'

There was an explosion of thunder.

'What do you want?' stammered Arnold.

'I want what is mine!' hissed the compost heap. 'This land you call yours belongs to me! I am the compost creature, the lord and master of this place! You must all leave it right now!'

'And if we don't?' Zoola challenged.

'I will return tomorrow night,' the compost creature threatened, 'and if you are still here, I will fill this house with a stink so bad that you will *have* to leave! If you're foolish enough to stay, I will cover you with mould so that you crumble into the earth. I am the enemy of all good things. So clear off!'

'I WANT WHAT IS MINE!' HISSED THE COMPOST HEAP

The compost heap moved away from the window and disappeared into the darkness as rain started to pelt down. The Hubbard family was too shocked to speak. Frogwarble was the first to move. She fluttered through the broken window and out into the rain. If Frogwarble was brave enough to go out, then so was I. I tip-toed through the back door, my nerves tingling like the overland telegraph. Frogwarble landed on some red clay not far away. When I stooped to pick her up, I noticed that there were tracks, deep grooves in the clay, softened by the rain. They were tyre tracks – three of them side by side. They led to the loungeroom window, then away down the hill.

I smelt something fishy – and it wasn't just compost.

'What's going on here?' a voice demanded, almost scaring the whiskers off me. I looked up to see Tito Graffito and his daughters, Pommy and Terri. Arnold, having recovered from his shock, stuck his head through the broken window.

'Did you find anything, Frank?' he yelled.

'Yeah!' I answered. 'I found three Graffitos!'

'So they *are* behind it all!' he growled. 'Just wait till they cop a bellyful of Zoola's ju-jitsu!'

Tito replied, 'Hold your horses, you pumpkin's pimple! We didn't come here to cause trouble. When we heard your windows smash we came here to see if you were all right. Of course I should have realised that the Hubbards wouldn't show any gratitude! Come on Pommy and Terri, let's go home!'

'That's right, crawl off!' yelled Butternut and Windsor.

'Just a moment!' I said to Arnold. 'I know who's at the bottom of all this and it's not the Graffitos. If we all work together we should be able to conquer the compost heap. What do you say?'

'Well...' Arnold began cautiously, 'if Frank's right, then I apologise. Would you... er... like to come in out of the rain?'

'All right,' said Tito suspiciously, 'but if Zoola tries her ju-jitsu on me, I'll call the cops!'

The Graffitos entered the Hubbard household, a thing which no Graffito had done since 1932 (when one fell through the roof while pouring mashed potato down the chimney). Gingerly, the Hubbard twins shook hands with the Graffito twins.

'We're all here Frank,' said Arnold. 'What are we going to do about the compost heap?'

'Jab it with a pitchfork!' cried Pommy.

'Shoot the manure out of it!' added Terri.

'No you don't!' scowled Zoola. 'That filthy thing's wearing my satins and I don't want them shot full of holes.'

'This is my plan,' I began. 'All we need are seven pumpkins, some carving knives and some candles.'

'Whatever you say!' Zoola nodded. 'We can rely on you, Frank.'

'And we'll have to cut up all your curtains,' I added.

Tito Graffito burst out laughing. 'Good on you, Frank! You're one member of the Hubbard family I could grow to like!'

The next night I stood in the backyard as bait for the compost creature. Every light in the Hubbards' house had been switched off. Frogwarble, who could see well in the dark, sat in the crown of my hat, ready to raise the alarm the moment she saw anything nasty.

'Boobook!' she hooted.

A strong smell of compost filled the air. The creature was approaching. I tried whistling, to settle my jangling nerves. The stink grew stronger and stronger. Suddenly, out of the darkness emerged a mountain of rotting rubbish and satin. It looked twice as big and ugly as it had the night before.

'Out of my way swagman!' hissed the compost creature in its mouldy voice. 'I have to deal with the Hubbards!'

'They've left!' I said. 'You scared them off.'

'Really?' it hissed. 'Then what are *you* doing here?'

'The Hubbards wanted me to give you a farewell present. It's in the pumpkin shed.'

'I hope you're not trying to trick me!' warned the compost creature, 'because if you are, I'll suck you up and keep you inside me till you rot!'

I led the compost creature to the shed. The creature had no arms so I opened the door for it, then leapt out of the way. When the compost heap saw what was inside the shed it started quaking and quivering.

'THE HUBBARDS WANTED ME TO GIVE YOU A FAREWELL PRESENT'

'Get away from me, you monsters!' it cried.

Seven hideous monsters leered at the compost heap. They had no bodies, just big floating heads with gaping mouths and terrible jagged teeth. Their triangle-eyes glowed fiercely in the dark. As they bobbed to and fro, they cackled in an evil way:

Floating pumpkin-heads are we!
Compost heaps we eat for tea!

With a howl of terror, the compost creature backed away clumsily. The pumpkin-heads mocked it with their blazing eyes and deathly grins. Frogwarble hooted excitedly.

'Leave me alone, you pumpkin-heads!' cried the compost creature, trying to escape but going round in circles. I heard strange creaky noises coming from under the layers of compost. The pumpkin-heads advanced menacingly towards the heap.

'Go away!' it shrieked. 'Go away!'

In a panic, the heap toppled over on to its side. Even in the darkness I could see that this was not a proper compost heap. There were three wheels underneath. A small door opened in the side of the heap and out struggled two familiar people.

'You absolute idiot, Doggo!' cursed Miss Blighter. 'You can't even pedal a tricycle properly!'

'*You* try pedalling a fake compost heap around!' Doggo protested. 'This is the stupidest idea you've ever had!'

'Shut your face!' snarled Miss Blighter. 'If it weren't for you panicking we would have scared the Hubbards away for good. Now you've ruined everything! You're fired, Doggo! Fired!'

The pumpkin-heads put a stop to the argument as they formed an evil circle around the two tricksters:

Floating pumpkin-heads are we!
We'll eat you, just wait and see!

'Please don't hurt me, pumpkin-heads!' snivelled Doggo. 'It's all Miss Blighter's fault. She wanted to scare the Hubbards off their property so she could expand the factory on to it.'

'Hold your tongue, Doggo!' snapped Miss Blighter.

'So we stole the real compost heap, then built a fake one on an ice-cream tricycle.'

'Quiet, Doggo, or I'll chocolate-coat you!'

The pumpkin-heads howled ferociously. Miss Blighter and Doggo fled back to the factory like two dogs with fireworks tied to their tails. The pumpkin-heads laughed uproariously:

Floating pumpkin-heads are we!
Don't come back, or dinner you'll be!

Frogwarble hooted happily and I replied:

You can't make me fret or faint
'Cause floating pumpkin-heads you ain't!

The members of the Hubbard family and the Graffito family put down the pumpkin-heads. They were really jack-o'-lanterns, hollowed-out pumpkins with gruesome faces and candles glowing inside. They seemed to be floating because the Hubbards and Graffitos were dressed in black capes made of curtain material, so it was impossible to see them in the dark. Arnold, Zoola, Windsor, Butternut, Tito, Pommy and Terri tossed back their black hoods and cackled in their best pumpkin-head voices.

'How about that!' said Arnold. 'Frank's idea worked! We conquered the colossal compost heap of Nar Nar Goon!'

'I reckon the Hubbards and the Graffitos make a good team!' said Tito.

'Let's hear it for Uncle Frank!' whooped Butternut.

Pommy asked, 'Can he be our Uncle Frank too?'

'Why not?' said Zoola. 'The whole world should have an Uncle Frank!'

And I blushed as they gave me three cheers, then took me inside to share some pumpkin wine and drink a toast to the night of the pumpkin-heads.

It was hard bidding farewell to the Hubbards and the Graffitos. Frogwarble and I had enjoyed family life but we decided it was time to leave when the families started feuding again. For the Hubbards and Graffitos both agreed that even though it was good to get along with neighbours, it was feuding that made life more interesting.

I walked out of Nar Nar Goon with Frogwarble asleep in the crown of my hat. It wasn't until the end of the day that I realised my boots had been mended. When I took them off, I found a note in one. It read:

Boulderbuster best beware!
Pumpkin-heads are everywhere!

But to this day I've never met another pumpkin-head.

NIGEL SWEET, TALL, SKINNY AND FUSSY,
WAS PHOTOGRAPHING A LADY SITTER

The Cologne Ranger

Some people hate having their picture taken. As soon as someone points a camera at them, they hide their faces, run away or start chucking things. But I love being photographed. That was why I was in Victoria, heading for the country town of Poowong. I had heard about a Poowong photographer called Nigel Sweet, who was supposed to be the best in Australia. His photographs made people look ten years younger than they really were. Grey hairs looked blond in Sweet's pictures and wrinkly old prune-faces were miraculously turned into smooth, fresh plums. No wonder he was so popular with people in the acting profession.

Since it was the middle of spring, the ground was green and damp. Beside the road to Poowong was a ditch full of water. To prepare myself for the photograph, I washed my face and hair in the ditch, then curled my beard with some bees' wax.

'Pretty flash, eh?' I said to Frogwarble, as she splashed about in the water. After spending a few minutes preening herself she looked as handsome as an owl could look.

All neat and scrubbed up, we swaggered along the road, past a sign which read, 'POOWONG – DANCING CAPITAL OF AUSTRALIA'. Another sign read, 'POOWONG DANCERS USE AND RECOMMEND POOZENOFF'S PATENT PERFUME – FOR *HAPPY* ARMPITS'.

I was just about to read a third sign when I received a rude shock. Screaming out of Poowong, on the wrong side of the road, was a baker's van. At the wheel, a grim-faced, grey-haired bloke sat with his hand pressed hard on the horn. Realising that this speed-demon had no intention of slowing down, I dived out of the way, not caring much where I landed, so long as it was well away from the van's burning wheels. I somersaulted into a ditch, where I was surrounded by frogs who started croaking angrily. But they weren't half as angry as me. I shook my fists and shouted some ungentlemanly words at the van driver, who was already well on his way to the next town.

SCREAMING OUT OF POOWONG, ON THE WRONG SIDE OF THE ROAD, WAS A BAKER'S VAN

'If ever I catch up with you,' I yelled, 'I'll clang your head between your hub caps!'

In spite of our narrow escape Frogwarble was more concerned about a bread roll which rested in the middle of the road. It must have fallen from the van. I got up, wrung out the ditch water from my coat, hat and blanket, then pocketed the bread roll. There was no sense in wasting good food.

If we hurried we would still be able to reach Nigel Sweet's studio before closing time. After getting our photographs we could go about finding a place to spend the night. It had been a hard day's walking and I badly needed some rest. Perhaps that was why I felt so irritated when a policeman stopped me.

'Who might you be, sir?' the very gruff, very fat policeman asked.

'Frank Boulderbuster's the name,' I replied. 'Gentleman of the road and proud visitor to Poowong.'

'Is that so, Mr Boulderbuster?' said the policeman. 'Well, I'm Sergeant Mullet of the Poowong police force, and I've got a nose like a bloodhound's. I can smell out criminals.'

'That must be difficult in a town where everybody uses Poozenoff's patent perfume,' I said.

'Not really, Mr Boulderbuster. You see, I've spent ten years training my nose. That's five years for each nostril. Now I can smell a criminal at a hundred paces.'

'Then I suggest you sniff out the driver of the baker's van that nearly knocked me down,' I said, 'because criminals like that make Australian roads unsafe.'

'We'll deal with that later,' rumbled Sergeant Mullet. 'First, empty out your pockets and unroll that blanket on your back.'

He searched through my belongings, including a jar of jam, some flour, a few coins and the bread roll.

'Nothing suspicious here,' he remarked, sounding disappointed, 'but I notice you have an owl with you. Is that your accomplice in crime?'

'Of course not!' I scoffed. 'She's never committed a crime in her life!'

'So, you prefer to work alone, do you? Come on, let's take off that false beard!'

The rotund Sergeant Mullet yanked my newly-waxed beard with all his might. I yelped loudly and, with a look of deep embarrassment, the Sergeant let go.

'Cripes, I'm sorry, mate!' he stammered.

'You duck-billed, dingo-witted drongo!' I cursed. 'I ought to pull your nincompoopish nose right off your fat face!'

'I made a mistake!' he moaned. 'I thought you were wearing false whiskers. You see, I sniffed you out as a criminal.'

'Then get your nose fixed! I'm a swagman, not a criminal. Can't you see that?'

'Ahh!' smiled the Sergeant, tapping his nose. 'Never mind what I see. This criminal we're hunting is a master of disguises. Even disguised himself as the dog on the tuckerbox once. So, our eyes aren't much use to us on this case. It's our noses that are doing the work. The trained police nose will be the undoing of this criminal.'

'I've never heard so much rubbish in my life! How can criminals smell any different to other people?'

'This criminal is a bit of a namby-pamby,' confided Sergeant Mullet. 'He always wears Titman's tinted toilet-water on his face.'

'Titman's tinted toilet-water!' I gasped. 'Then you can only be referring to one person – The Cologne Ranger!'

'That's right!' said Sergeant Mullet, 'But how could a simple bloke like you know of a classy jewel thief like the Cologne Ranger?'

'We grew up in the same town. I knew him when he was just the toilet-water terror of Triambelong. He was a thief, a con man and an all-round little stinker. I'd put jumping ants in his sleeping bag any day.'

Sergeant Mullet sighed. 'We just can't catch the sweet-scented scoundrel, even though we've got our best noses on the job. We know he's somewhere in Poowong because, in the last few days, jewellery has been disappearing from under our very noses. Some of it was traced in Melbourne yesterday, but we can't work out how the Cologne Ranger smuggles it out of town. Everybody who comes in or goes out gets searched. It's been very hard on the police, especially with the Poowong Dancing Contest tomorrow.'

'I expect you've got a lot of strange people coming into town,' I said.

Sergeant Mullet nodded sadly. 'It's getting so as the Poowong police force hasn't got time to rehearse its ballet number. We're doing *The Nutcracker Suite* this year.'

'Good for you!' I said. 'Are you playing the sugar-plum fairy?'

'Don't be stupid!' growled Sergeant Mullet. 'The plum parts always go to the Chief Inspector.' He gave another sigh. 'I only hope we catch the Cologne Ranger before the finals. It's so hard to find a pongy pilferer in a town addicted to Poozenoff's patent perfume. It's a bit like trying to sniff out a rose in a field of lilacs. That's why there's a reward of a thousand dollars for his capture.'

Sergeant Mullet pointed to a 'WANTED' poster stuck to a Poozenoff's billboard. The face on the poster was ugly. No wonder the Cologne Ranger was always disguising himself. Under his false whiskers and make-up was a nasty, thin face with black hair combed behind the right ear. The left ear was a mystery in that it was not there. Nobody knew what had happened to it, but the Cologne Ranger had been without a left ear for as long as people could remember.

One thousand dollars for the capture of a one-eared villain was more money than I had ever seen before, and certainly more money than I needed, but I couldn't help thinking about it as I said good-bye to Sergeant Mullet and headed for Nigel Sweet's photographic studio.

Sweet might have been the best photographer in Australia but he was also the rudest. I don't mean that he took rude pictures (you'd never catch a modest bloke like me posing for rude pictures) but he was rude to his customers. He never asked them politely to say 'Cheese!'. He just told them to flash their teeth and try not to look too much like a Melbourne Cup favourite.

Nigel Sweet, tall, skinny and fussy, was photographing a lady sitter when I called. She was one of the smartest-looking ladies I had ever seen but it didn't make any difference to Sweet.

'Don't open your mouth so wide, Miss Wackett!' he stormed. 'I feel like a shark's dentist.'

'Sorry, Sweetie!' said Miss Wackett. 'Should I put on more make-up?'

'No, Miss Wackett!' replied Sweet, firmly. 'You've already had more coats than the Sydney Harbour Bridge. Now, keep still and try not to show too many wrinkles.'

'They're not wrinkles!' Miss Wackett flushed. 'They're laugh-lines.'

'My dear Miss Wackett, *nothing* is that funny!'

There was a click and the whole ordeal was over. Miss Wackett, who had been sticking her large chest out like a Major Mitchell cockatoo, relaxed. Sweet, wiping his brow with a frilly hankie soaked in Poozenoff's patent perfume, turned to me.

'And what do *you* want?' he demanded. 'I expect you're also entering this ridiculous Dancing Contest and you want me to take your picture for the *Poowong Pictorial*?'

'I only just heard about it!' I protested.

'But everybody knows about the Poowong Dancing Contest!' insisted Miss Wackett. 'Dancers come from all over Australia to compete for the famous Poowong Cup. I'm from Mudgee myself and I intend to take that Cup back home with me.'

'Do you like dancing, then?' I asked.

'*Do I like dancing?*' shrieked Miss Wackett, imitating a cockatoo again. 'I'll have you know, I'm Princess Googie Wackett, the sensational spider-dancer of Mudgee!'

'Well, I'm just plain Frank Boulderbuster,' I said, 'and the only reason I'm here is to get my picture taken.'

Sweet fluttered his hand at some photos decorating the walls of his shop.

'Here you see some fine examples of my work!' he boasted. 'They may look dull to you but they're a great improvement on real life, take my word for it. All of these people have entered the Contest.'

There was Madame Dugite the snake-dancer, Sam and Moose the dancing fishmongers with their famous marine waltz, and Bluey Pike the shuffling baker.

'My money's on Bluey Pike,' said Sweet. 'What he can do with a pair of dancing shoes and a cottage loaf would make your eyes pop out!'

'Don't be so sure!' said Miss Wackett. 'Old Bluey's not looking too well these days, and his poppy-seed shuffle isn't what it used to be. Poor dear! But just wait till you see my spider-dance! I've got a brand new costume and I'm going to wear my two-thousand-dollar gold earrings. Mr Sweet, could you be an angel and take a picture of me wearing them?'

'Very well!' said Sweet.

Suddenly Miss Wackett screamed loud enough to wake a politician. I thought Frogwarble might have frightened her, as she sometimes has this effect on people. But Miss Wackett was staring into her handbag.

'They've been stolen!' she squawked. 'My two-thousand-dollar earrings have been pinched! They must have been taken last night at the dancing rehearsals, right in front of the Poowong police force!' She looked angry. 'I knew it was a mistake for *all* of them to dance "The Waltz of the Flowers".'

'You careless thing, Miss Wackett!' snapped Sweet. 'If you hadn't gas-bagged about those earrings, this dreadful thing wouldn't have happened.'

'Fair crack of the whip!' I said, hoping that Miss Wackett appreciated that I was sticking up for her. 'She wasn't careless, she was just unlucky. I know the thief who took them and he's sly enough to steal the gold fillings out of your teeth while you sneeze. Miss Wackett is not to blame.'

Miss Wackett looked at me with blue, twinkly eyes. I smiled back. If it hadn't been for Sweet butting in, I might have heard little love-birds singing in my earholes.

'You'll have to leave now!' said Sweet. 'I'm shutting up shop.'

'What about my photograph?' I said.

'Sorry, but I'm too overcome with shock to work. Anyway, I'm sure it's past closing time.'

He reached into his waistcoat pocket and searched for something. His face dropped as he withdrew his empty hand.

'My gold watch! It's been stolen!'

Turning the same shade of mauve as his hankie, he collapsed into a chair.

'It was a birthday present from my mummy.'

'You poor love,' fussed Miss Wackett. 'It must have meant a lot to you.'

'Frankly, I couldn't stand the thing,' admitted Sweet. 'It was a nasty, horrid watch – but mummy'll kill me if she finds out I've lost it!'

Miss Wackett looked at me urgently. 'Mr Boulderbuster ... *Frank*... you know of the thief who's been robbing us. Do you think you can crack the case for us?'

I hesitated, then said, 'Don't worry. I'll crack it, Miss Wackett!'

Twinkly eyes can make you say silly things.

That night, Frogwarble and I made ourselves comfortable under a stringybark tree near the Poowong Sports Ground. I lit a fire and cooked my jam damper. Frogwarble was making a bit of a song and dance about not having enough to eat, probably because fewer flies were buzzing around me since I had taken my afternoon wash. To quieten her down, I took the bread roll out of my pocket and gave it to her. Then I gobbled my damper and fell asleep, to dream of being Miss Wackett's partner in her amazing spider-dance. I slept well and didn't wake till morning, when I felt somebody putting something on my wrists.

'Wakey, wakey, Mr Boulderbuster!'

It was the gruff voice of Sergeant Mullet. Wearily, I saw him standing over me. When I tried to wipe the dust from my eyes I found that my wrists had been handcuffed.

'That's a mean sort of joke to play on a bloke,' I said.

'No joke!' smiled Sergeant Mullet. 'I've sniffed you out and you're coming with me to the lock-up!'

'Give me one good reason why I should!'

'I'll give you two!' the joyful Sergeant said.

Then he pointed to two gold earrings in the grass alongside me.

No matter how many times I told Sergeant Mullet that I hadn't stolen Miss Wackett's earrings, he wouldn't believe me. And who could blame him? He seemed convinced I was the Cologne Ranger in an ingenious disguise and believed the best place for me was behind bars in the Poowong Penitentiary.

I sat in the cold, grey cell feeling miserable for three reasons; miserable because I hadn't eaten for hours, miserable because Miss Wackett would think I was a rotten thief and miserable because Frogwarble had flown off and left me all alone.

Humming some tunes from *The Nutcracker Suite*, Sergeant Mullet brought a plate of delicious-smelling sausages in batter to the door of my cell. He ate one so quickly that it was easy to see how he had achieved a belly like a bag full of jellyfish.

'Great tucker!' he burped. 'You can have some, if you admit you're the Cologne Ranger.'

'For the hundredth time,' I groaned, 'I'm not the Cologne Ranger. I'm Frank Boulderbuster, the best and, right now, the *hungriest* swagman in Australia.'

'Where did you hide the watch you stole from Mr Sweet?' he persisted, not listening to a word I'd said.

'Sergeant Mullet, a bloke with a nose as good as yours should be able to tell that I'm not the Cologne Ranger. I don't smell a bit like Titman's tinted toilet-water.'

'All I can smell right now is these delicious snags in batter,' he said. 'I'll bring them back when you're ready to tell the truth.'

He thumped off, leaving me feeling hungrier than ever. If ever I got out of there, I vowed I would catch the Cologne Ranger and tan his perfumed hide. It was his fault that I was there. He must have planted those earrings on me, knowing I'd cop the blame.

'Boobook!'

Frogwarble's familiar cry echoed through the cell. I had never heard a sweeter sound. She was perched between the bars of the window above me. In her beak she held a bread roll, like the one I had fed her the previous night. It made my mouth water and I was more grateful than a bullfrog in a summer shower when

Frogwarble dropped the roll into my cell. The smell of freshly baked bread was almost as good as the smell of damper. I took a huge bite.

Crunch!

Something besides flour and milk had gone into this bread roll. As I scraped away the bread, I found a gold watch in the centre. On the back was engraved, 'To Nigel, Happy Fortieth Birthday, from Mummy'. So this was Nigel Sweet's stolen watch – and it was still ticking! I tried to make sense of it all. What would a watch be doing in the middle of a bread roll? Of course! This was how the Cologne Ranger had been smuggling the stolen jewels out of Poowong! He was hiding them in bread rolls and driving them out in a baker's van. And that was how the earrings had been discovered next to me. They must have been in the bread roll that fell out of the baker's van. Frogwarble had eaten the roll and left the earrings behind for Sergeant Mullet to discover.

'All I have to do is explain this to Sergeant Mullet and I'll be a free bloke again!' I said to Frogwarble.

She held her head to one side and gazed at me in doubt. She was right, of course. The story was so incredible, Sergeant Mullet would be as likely to believe me as believe that there were sugar-plum fairies at the bottom of his garden. Let's face it, I was stuck there.

'You'd better think of a way to get me out of here!' I told Frogwarble. 'After all, you put me in here by leaving those jewels alongside me. Next time, don't leave anything on your dinner plate!'

Frogwarble stared at me with her yellow eyes. It was her hypnotic eyes that gave me a crazy escape plan. Since I was desperate to get out of there, I decided to try it. Grabbing the bars of my cell and shaking them, I yelled out that I was now willing to tell the truth. Quick as a cat with its tail on fire, Sergeant Mullet appeared at the door.

'So, you've decided to be sensible!' smiled Sergeant

'SLEEPY!' REPEATED SERGEANT MULLET

Mullet. 'You can start by telling me where you hid Mr Sweet's gold watch.'

'It's right here!' I said, dangling the watch before his tiny blue eyes. 'If you look closely you can see where his mum had it engraved for him.'

'Hold the blinking thing still!' barked Sergeant Mullet.

'Can you read the time on it?' I murmured, tonelessly.

'Of course I can!' he huffed. 'Now, hold it still!'

'See how it shines!' I whispered. 'Keep your eyes on it. Watch the watch. Do you know what time it is? It's bedtime. You are sleepy!'

'Sleepy!' repeated Sergeant Mullet.

'You are asle-e-e-e-e-p!'

His eyelids drooped. He looked asleep all right. It had taken so little time to hypnotise Sergeant Mullet that I suspected he might have been tricking me. I tried a little test.

'You will obey me!' I droned.

'I will obey you!' mumbled Sergeant Mullet.

'You are a great stupid nong!' I said.

'I am a great stupid nong,' recited the Sergeant.

'Your head contains more cotton wool than a padded bra.'

'My head contains more cotton wool than a padded bra.'

'Your belly is as big as a national park.'

'My belly is as big as a national park.'

'You could grow gum trees in your belly button.'

'I could grow gum trees in my belly button.'

I was beginning to enjoy myself. Now for some *real* fun.

'You will start dancing right now!' I ordered.

I was expecting to see him dance a sleepy little shuffle, but my hypnotic powers were stronger than I thought. Sergeant Mullet's little eyes opened wide. He raised his chubby arms. Then, lifting the heels of his highly polished policeman's boots, he twisted. I had never seen anybody twist so well.

'Let's twist again,' he sang, 'like we did last summer...'

Before he exhausted himself I tried the supreme test. Now I would find out just how hypnotised he really was!

'You will unlock the cell door!' I ordered, gently.

'I will unlock the cell door!' repeated Sergeant Mullet, dreamily twisting over to my cell. He slipped the key in the lock, opened the door and bowed to me as I crept out. Suddenly he grabbed me. My heart sank as I realised he must have been fooling me all along. I was expecting him to bawl in my earhole but instead he twittered, 'All of the blooms were there, dancing the Waltz of the Flowers...' He held me close. He didn't want to throttle me, he wanted to *waltz* with me! *One*, two, three, *one*, two, three; we glided around the Poowong Penitentiary. Sergeant Mullet had a look of great joy on his round, pink face. I hoped like mad that he wouldn't wake up to find me clutched in his arms. Fortunately, I managed to squeeze out of his strong grasp. I gave him a hatstand in my place but not before I grabbed a hat, coat and scarf from it. Wearing this disguise, I left the Poowong Penitentiary to Sergeant Mullet, who was waltzing with the hatstand as if it were the most graceful dancing partner he had ever had.

I persuaded Frogwarble to leave me for a while, since if she had perched on my hat she would have ruined my disguise. Wrapping the scarf around the bottom half of my face, I scurried down the main street of Poowong. I was alone. The place was clean but deserted, like a ghost town kept by tidy ghosts. Nigel Sweet's studio was shut, the Town Hall, post office and general store were shut, and the big oven at Bluey Pike's bakery was dead. The raucous sound of a bush band drifted down the street, reminding me that today was the day of the Poowong Dancing Contest. I had to go, since the Cologne Ranger was bound to be there.

I followed the music to the Sports Ground where I had spent the previous night. But the place was impossible to recognise. The small grandstand was covered in purple banners: 'THE POOWONG DANCING CONTEST, PROUDLY SPONSORED BY POOZENOFF'S PATENT PERFUME'. A band of Poozenoff's marching girls raised their arms high, to show off their happy armpits. In one corner of the ground some traditional morris-dancers hopped and skipped around a 1954 Morris Minor. In another corner, the Poowong police force performed *The Nutcracker Suite*, sadly having to use a police dog as a stand-in because Sergeant Mullet was unable to take part. There were dancers who made your hair stand on end. They were twisting, twirling, heel-and-toeing, sliding, spinning, dosey-doe-ing. Sam and Moose, the famous dancing fishmongers, did their amazing marine waltz dressed in flippers, goggles and snorkels. It was very graceful but not as popular as Madame Dugite the snake-dancer, who did her act in a tiny costume made of crêpe paper.

Although I wanted to watch Madame Dugite's startling act I pushed my way through the crowd, trying to sniff the Cologne Ranger, but smelling instead a vast sea of Poozenoff's patent perfume. At the hub of all the activity was the Poowong Cup – the trophy which dancers all over Australia longed to have on their mantelpieces. Suddenly, my nostrils detected something. There was no mistaking the aroma of Titman's tinted toilet-water. It was coming from a gentleman who stood with his back to me. He was edging towards the trophy. So here was the Cologne Ranger, planning to make his most daring robbery yet! Before I could get any closer, I was mobbed by a cheering crowd.

'Ladies and blokes!' crackled a voice from a loudspeaker stuck up a stringybark. 'Let's give a real

Poowong welcome to the mysterious Princess Googie Wackett from Mudgee, who is going to perform her sensational, scandalizing and slightly saucy *spider-dance*!'

Confused by the jostling crowd, I staggered this way and that. Finally, someone trod on the end of my scarf and I tumbled into the dancing arena. To a trumpet fanfare, Miss Wackett appeared, dressed in a black spider outfit, with false arms sticking out of her sides and feather dusters bobbing around on her hat. She edged towards me, chucking streamers at me. I guessed this was supposed to be her web. Hoping she wouldn't recognise me, I started to play along. She was the spider and I was her fly. I shook my backside, flapped my arms then circled as fast as I could manage. Suddenly, I was dancing with Miss Wackett as I had done in my dreams.

SUDDENLY I WAS DANCING WITH MISS WACKETT AS I HAD DONE IN MY DREAMS

All eyes were on us.

Fortunately, *my* eyes were on the mysterious gentleman who lurked near the trophy. I saw him snatch the Cup from its stand. Somehow, I had to prove that this was the Cologne Ranger up to his dirty doings, and I had to prove it fast!

There was one more trick up my sleeve. I danced with renewed vigour.

'Look at that old codger go!' I heard someone yell.

'He looks like a barefoot tight-rope walker on barbed wire!'

With great effort I performed some magic steps. Right foot in, right foot out, right foot in, then shake it all about. When I got to the hokey-kokey part black storm clouds rolled across the sky. I turned myself around and a huge pink streak of lightning split the sky in half.

A few spots of rain began to fall. Then it showered. Then it pelted down. I danced on, thanking my old mother for teaching me her rain dance. The rain fell in buckets. It fell in sheets. It even fell on Madame Dugite's crêpe-paper costume and washed it away. But most of all, it fell on the gentleman wearing Titman's tinted toilet-water, the bloke that everyone thought was Bluey Pike. It was now safe to take off my disguise. I tossed aside the hat, scarf and coat.

'It's you! gasped Miss Wackett. 'You're the swaggie who pinched my earrings!'

'No, Miss Wackett!' I cried. 'The pungent plunderer who's been robbing everybody is standing over there!'

I pointed at Bluey Pike. As we watched, his face seemed to change. In the rain his hair went from grey to black. White trickles ran down his forehead. Make-up washed away, revealing a mean, thin face. But the most horrible thing of all was that his left ear slid down his neck, then dropped on to the ground. There it lay, not a real ear at all but a false one made from bread dough. As the rain pelted down, the fake ear went mushy and dissolved.

'Great bounding bandicoots!' a policeman in a tutu cried. 'It's the Cologne Ranger!'

'Grab him!' his dance partner cried.

But the Cologne Ranger was as sly as he was smelly. He tossed the Poowong Cup at the approaching police, who fell like fence posts in a termite plague. Cackling evilly, he bolted through the crowd. And he would have got away too if it hadn't been for Sergeant Mullet. Just as the Cologne Ranger broke free of the crowd he collided with the fat Sergeant waltzing with the hatstand. Sergeant Mullet had waltzed all the way from the Poowong Penitentiary to the Sports Ground under the spell of my hypnosis. But the collision woke him up instantly.

'Don't move, Cologne Ranger!' he yelled. 'I've got you covered with this... er... hatstand.'

Naturally, the Cologne Ranger tried to escape but a blow from the hatstand made him change his mind. Cursing and muttering, he was led away by Sergeant Mullet, who boasts to this day that he is the only policeman who has ever used a piece of furniture to catch a criminal.

That day was the luckiest day of Sergeant Mullet's life. Not only did he collect the one-thousand-dollar reward for catching the Cologne Ranger, but he also got second prize in the Poowong Dancing Contest for his novelty waltz, winning for himself a year's supply of Poozenoff's patent perfume.

The Cologne Ranger wasn't so lucky. His plan had been well and truly foiled. As I suspected, he had disguised himself as a baker in order to rob the Poowong people and bake their valuables into bread rolls so he could sneak them out of town. At the bakery we found a whole tray of rolls containing rings, cufflinks and brooches. We also found the real Bluey Pike. The poor bloke had been bound and gagged for five days, but the thing that upset him most was missing the Dancing Contest.

It was some contest. For the first year ever, the judges awarded the Poowong Cup to two dancers – Miss Wackett and Frank Boulderbuster.

'Isn't it just gorgeous?' cried Miss Wackett, emptying a bottle of pink champagne into the cup. 'We'll have to share it, you know.'

'The champagne or the Cup?' I asked.

'Why, *both*, of course!' she giggled.

Frogwarble perched on the Cup's brim as I took a drink. I had never tasted pink champagne before and don't mind if I never do again. It tasted stranger than Northern Territory beer.

'There you go!' laughed Miss Wackett, as I screwed up my face.

'But how can we share the Cup?' I asked.

For a few moments, she looked lost in thought. Then she said, 'We'll have to share a mantelpiece to keep it on. And if you have a mantelpiece you really need a house to go with it.'

'You mean we should share a house?' I gulped.

'We'd need to share a wedding first,' explained Miss Wackett, quite matter-of-factly.

Frogwarble, on the rim of the Cup, gave me a cheeky wink.

'Excuse me, Miss Wackett, but I really must be going,' I said. 'Please keep the Cup. I hope it will remind you of me.'

'Farewell then, Frank,' she sniffed, 'but what can you take that will remind you of me?'

Suddenly, Nigel Sweet appeared with his camera.

'Smile, you two!' he ordered.

There was a blinding flash.

'What a nice couple!' clucked Sweet, removing the plate from his camera. 'But it would never work. Never!'

As Frogwarble fell into the champagne and Miss Wackett made a full-scale fuss about it, I realised Nigel Sweet was right.

I picked up the photograph the next morning, then went on my way, with my blanket strapped to my back, my coat pockets full of flour and jam, and my owl perched firmly in the crown of my hat.

So here I am today, still travelling the roads of Australia. Every now and then I look at the photograph of Miss Wackett and me with the Cup and think of what might have been. I might have got married, raised a mob of little Boulderbusters and slept under the same roof every night. In the evenings, I often ask Frogwarble if I made the right decision. She just hoots lazily, eating one last fly for supper.

And I look up at the only roof I could never grow tired of – the winking stars of the glorious Southern Cross.

About the Author

Born in 1959 Doug MacLeod contributed a monthly column of poetry to the Melbourne *Age* when he was twelve. His first book, *Hippopotabus* was published when he was sixteen.

For eighteen months he compered the ABC's rock music program, *Rave*, and interviewed most of Australia's best rock bands. Besides his many children's books, he has written children's and adult scripts for radio and television, including an ABC radio current affairs program for teenagers which he also presented, as well as scripts for various fringe theatre groups.

In 1985 he joined Express Australia, the youth media bureau in Melbourne, and worked on exhibitions, radio broadcasts and other projects for International Youth Year. He also helps to edit *Puffinalia*, the magazine of the Australian Puffin Club.

Tales of Tuttle

Professor Tuttle is an absent-minded genius who's forever trying to invent the perfect machine. So far, his inventions have been anything but perfect – but the Professor *never* gives up. He has some hair-raising adventures with two robots called Glube and Grok, a Parcel-wrapping Machine, and the dreaded Pink Shrink (a hypersonic particle reducer).

Luckily his friends, Miss Purdie, Old Bill and MacTavish, are usually there to help him out. But if you find yourself wrapped up like a birthday present or chased by a pair of bionic teeth, you can be sure that Professor Tuttle is in town.

The Fed Up Family Album

'We're doomed, we're sunk, we're deadi-bones!' moaned gloomy Uncle Jeffrey Jaspar Jones, one of the many uncles, aunts, cousins and other oddities that fill this album. The Fed Up Family is a family unlike any other. There is Cousin Lurch who donned skates for his wedding, and Aunt Clover McBreeze whose gaping jaws caused *the* Royal Scandal, and even a sabre-toothed family cat.

They say that every family has a skeleton in the cupboard. But *The Fed Up Family Album* digs up enough bones to make a full-sized Brontosaurus.

HEARD ABOUT THE PUFFIN CLUB?

. . . it's a way of finding out more about Puffin books and authors, of winning prizes (in competitions), sharing jokes, a secret code, and perhaps seeing your name in print! When you join you get a copy of our magazine, *Puffinalia*, sent to you four times a year, a badge and a membership book. For details of subscription and an application form, send a stamped addressed envelope to:

The Australian Puffin Club
Penguin Books Australia Limited
PO Box 257
Ringwood
Victoria 3134

and if you live in the UK, please write to

The Puffin Club Dept A
Penguin Books Limited
Bath Road
Harmondsworth
Middlesex UB7 ODA